A Flock in the Wilderness
Panda Books

Chi Zijian was born in Mohe on the Lantern Festival in 1964. She graduated from the Daxinganling Teachers School in 1984 and studied at the graduate-training class jointly sponsored by Beijing Normal University and Lu Xun Literature Institute. Since graduation in 1990 she's been working in the Heilongjiang Provincial Writers Association. She started her writing career in 1983 and became known for her *A Fairy Tale in North Pole Village* in 1986. She has published nearly four million characters. Her major works include the full-length novel *Under the Tree*, *In the Vast Country of the North* and *A Fairy Tale in North Pole Village*. She's now a member of the Chinese Writers Association.

A Flock in the Wilderness

Chi Zijian

Panda Books

First Edition 2005

ISBN 7-119-03664-5

© Foreign Languages Press, Beijing, China, 2005

Published by Foreign Languages Press

24 Baiwanzhuang Road, Beijing 100037, China

Website: http://www.flp.com.cn

E-mail Address: info@flp.com.cn

sales@flp.com.cn

Distributed by China International Book Trading Corporation

35 Chegongzhuang Xilu, Beijing 100044, China

P.O. Box 399, Beijing, China

Printed in the People's Republic of China

CONTENTS

CONTENTS

Editors' Note

WHEN the Cultural Revolution came to an end in 1976, especially after 1978 when China adopted the policy of reform and opening to the outside world, one tidal wave of creative writing after another has washed over the face of Chinese literature. Chinese women writers have added their indelible inscriptions to this New Age Literature. Their works present a good cross-section of life in China. Among these writers are Shen Rong, Wang Anyi, Zhang Jie, Cheng Naishan, Tie Ning, Lu Xing'er, Chi Li, Zhang Xin, Fang Fang, Chi Zijian, and Bi Shumin, to name only a few.

The late 1970s and the early 1980s was a period of literary renaissance, thanks to the relaxed political climate and growing democracy in China. Many women writers emerged, dealing with all kinds of subject matters and attracting widespread attention. The school of "wound literature" took shape, which mainly focuses on people's lives during and after the Cultural Revolution. Shen Rong's "At Middle Age" raises the problems of middle-aged professionals, who enter the new age with marks left on them by the Cultural Revolution and who have to divide their time between career and family and more often than not neglect one or the other. Cheng Naishan, perceptive, objective, penetrating, and compassionate, captivates her readers with stories about the lives and loves, the destinies and the emotional entanglements of the industrial and business families of China's metropolis, a class which has weathered political vicissitudes before and during the Cultural Revolution. "The Blue House," her representative work, is one such story describing the turmoil going through the Gu family, the former steel giant in Shanghai who owned the Blue House.

Women writers were truthful spokesmen for the youth who suffered during the Cultural Revolution. Problems of the young people of the time were frankly dealt with, such as their disrupted education; lack of interesting employment; the difficulties met with by boys and girls sent from town to the countryside; the low incomes and overcrowding which threaten to break up young couples' marriages; their mental confusion after the turbulent years in which traditions were thrown overboard and bureaucracy, nepotism and corruption were rampant. Zhang Jie's "Love Must Not Be Forgotten" had aroused considerable interest as well as much controversy. Boldly unconventional, idealistic and intensely romantic, the story sheds interesting light on the changes in the attitude to love in socialist China, still strongly influenced by feudal ideas about marriage at the time.

While reform was still dawning on the Chinese horizon, Zhang Jie captured the historic social changes of this mood of reform in her important novel, "Leaden Wings." First published in 1981 and an instant bestseller, the story has as its central theme the modernization of industry. The publication of this book aroused further controversy. Exposing various abuses and man-made obstacles to modernization, it came under fir. for "attacking socialism." But many readers welcomed it as painting a truthful picture of modern Chinese society of the time.

In the mid-1980s, seeking out and examining the roots of Chinese culture became the dominant trend, hence the term "root literature." Leading this trend was Wang Anyi's novella "Xiaobao Village," which dissects the rights and wrongs of traditional moral values by portraying what happens behind closed doors in a tiny village that is generally extolled as a paragon of humanity and justice. The author's rich choice of language and her profound grasp of the cultural life and nature of people in a small village, places "Xiaobao Village" on a par with Ah Cheng's "The Chess Master" and Han Shaogong's "Father."

Wang Anyi, who represents the writers whose formal education was disrupted by the Cultural Revolution knows from firsthand experience the problems of young people who have returned from communes to the cities. In her stories, a sense of humanism appears. She is not one simply to condemn or write off the 10 years of her generation lost because of the Cultural Revolution. In her creative world, authentic human feelings live through the traumatic days of the Cultural Revolution. They are perpetuated along with—perhaps in tandem with—the old class relations, with all their old prejudices, suspicions, and tolerances, too. Wang Anyi analyzes China with an imagination that seems nourished by both pre-revolutionary and post-revolutionary culture. Her stories are alive with such tensions and contrasts. Her stories "Lapse of Time" and "The Destination" have won literary prizes in China.

In the late 1980s, Neo-realism came in vogue in Chinese fiction, of which Chi Li, author of "Trials and Tribulations," and Fang Fang, who wrote "Landscape," are both hailed as founding members.

Chi Li is an active writer on the Chinese literary scene. Her stories, like the above-mentioned "Trials and Tribulations" and "Apart from Love," mostly focus on the female world, their love and marriage, though her attitude has nothing to do with feminism. The detailed and earthy descriptions conjure up a vivid picture of life in the late 1980s.

Fang Fang began by writing humorous stories, which are full of caustic and witty remarks. She then turned to stories about magic in which her characters summon up wind and rain like spirits. But she later changed her style again. She is sort of unpredictable, constantly surprising readers and critics because she does not confine herself to a certain style. One of the most popular female writers in present-day China, she is best known for her stories about urban life, with characters ranging from intellectuals to laborers. Her "Landscape" depicts the relationships between an illiterate docker and his nine children, and the hardships they endure in a raw struggle to survive.

During the transitional 1990s, New Age Literature came to an end. The transformation of social and economic patterns in China has given rise to multiple literary patterns with writers of various pursuits locked in a keenly contested competition. The principle of literature has changed from serving life to serving man's existence, and from presenting people's aspirations for life and the historical destiny of collectives to depicting ordinary people's existence in this world. Works by women writers started to describe the petty vexations of people working to earn and survive in the mundane world. Neo-realism, first appearing in the late 1980s and represented by Chi Li and Fang Fang, has developed to a new height. Chi Li's relatively recent stories, "To and Fro" and "Life Show," have presented a vivid, realistic picture of the life of women in the fast-changing Chinese society. Bi Shumin, a doctor-turned woman writer, focuses on specific social and economic phenomena, revealing the contradictions in modern society and the true nature of man in the face of the social and economic reforms in China. But her works don't just stop there. Her novella "An Appointment with Death" and full-length novel *The Red Prescription* aim for a broader philosophical meaning beyond the superficial implications of subjects like hospice care, life and death, drug use and rehabilitation.

Today, China's relaxed political climate and growing democracy have resulted in more truthful writing and a wider range of themes. Love, social injustice, the value of the individual, humanism and other subjects formerly taboo are being fearlessly tackled by women writers—often with an unabashed display of emotion.

As editors, we hope that this series of women writers' works, compiled and published by Foreign Languages Press, will open a door to the world of Chinese women writers and to the everyday life of ordinary Chinese, for our readers who are interested in Chinese literature and China as well.

The River Rolls By

EACH year, towards the end of September or at the beginning of October, a sort of "tear fish" as locals call it, swims down from the upper reaches of the Shichuan River, crying all the way.

Although still in a state of fatigue and excitement from the tortoise season that has just ended, the fishermen start to prepare their tackle as soon as they feel the coming of the first winter snow: for them it is imperative that they catch several tear fish, for only in this way can they feel worthy of the love of their wives and children, and of the year's harvest.

The tear fish is unique to the Shichuan River. Its body is oblate, its fin red and its scales blue, and it only appears after the first snow of each year, accompanied by sobs which resound throughout the river.

When tear fish are caught, actual tear drops are seen falling from their eyes, their red tails wagging slightly, the deep blue of their scales suffused with a sheen like delicate petals and their soft gills working like bellows. At this time, the fishermen's wives hasten to put them into big wooden basins, comforting them in a gentle tone: "There, there, do not cry any more;

there, there..." Sure enough, the tear fish stop crying and start to swim at ease in the basins, enjoying the unexpected warmth shown by the people. If you can bear the sorrowful sound of the water in early winter, there are good fish to be caught here.

As the tear fish usually come down from the upper reaches at the first dusk following the first snow, the fishermen prepare bonfires on the bank early in the afternoon, which from a distance look like many shining golden bowls. Local women have high cheek bones, almond-shaped eyes and thick lips. They walk with quick steps that greatly emphasise their fine motherly potential: as a complement to which they have very healthy appetites. They like to wear purplish blue or silvery grey scarves and always pull their hair in a bun no matter how young or old they are. Standing on the bank of the Shichuan River they resemble thick and straight black birches.

The fishermen have no idea from whence the Shichuan River springs. The only thing they know about it is that it flows here from the very far north. The river, which can not be described as wide, has a surface that lies as smooth and peaceful as a mirror. Even in the rainy season the river does not produce roaring waves, but there is an endless, lingering mist that rises out of the water and spreads to the woods on the banks. The Shichuan River bed must be sunk very deep.

It was late autumn and the wind was wantonly tearing away the withered tree leaves. Jixi, a sensitive woman at the age of seventy-eight, had already finished preparing for catching tear fish. She was skinny and hunch-backed and fond of dried berries and mushrooms. If you take a small boat down from the upper river and pass this small village called Ahjia, should you want to have a cup of fragrant tea, drop by Jixi's house. She keeps tobacco leaves prepared, the kind that men are fond of, all year round, and several long-stemmed bronze pipes lying in the cupboard in neat order. All you have to do is enjoy yourself.

It was never difficult to recognise Jixi among the villagers. If in Ahjia Village, you ran into a tall girl with a full figure, a high, straight nose and red lips walking down a muddy road and smelling of fresh fish, it could be none other than Jixi, her young self fifty years ago. She set her hair in the shape of a bun; had limpid eyes and white teeth; always wore a grey cloth dress in summer, which was so long that it almost touched the earth. She ate raw fish in a stylish way so loveable and pleasing to the eye that fishermen even liked to watch her when they suffered stomach cramps and could themselves take neither food nor water. The instant they saw Jixi's sharp teeth biting into the bright snow-white scales and the tender meat, sending out a magical, musical sound, they would yearn for food. Now it is very easy to meet her in Ahjia Village. If you see a hunch-backed old woman, her eyes bursting with the brightness of light bouncing off fish scales the moment she looks up, you can be sure that she is Jixi; an old one now.

The snow came quietly at five o'clock in the early morning. Jixi had nightmares that night and was cursing God on the sly when she heard a rustling sound from the window frames like that of fish scales being scraped away from the skin. No doubt it was snowing, the prelude to the coming of tear fish. Coldness, plus a fit of vehement coughing, had woken her completely. After putting on her clothes, she got up from the *kang**, lit the

---

* A *kang* bed is the central part of country dwellings. Built of brick, it houses a fire which is used to cook food and for heating in winter.

stove and placed two potatoes on an iron stand to roast. She
then lit an oil lamp and began to examine her net to make sure it
was in good condition. She tied one end of the net to a nail on
the wall, the other to the door handle. About ten or so metres
long, the net floated between the door and the wall like thin
mist, its silvery thread turning amber in the glow of the flickering lamp wick. Jixi was delighted as if smelling the aroma of
resin. The net was the work of her own hands, woven into a
mesh of average size, although her fingers were not as nimble
with the wooden shuttle as they once had been. In Ahjia Village, there was not one family that had not used a net produced
by her hand. When she was a girl, young and strong fishermen
would always bring back balls of snow-white thread from town
and ask her to weave all sizes of fishing nets. In return, they
would buy her scarves, ornaments and beautiful buttons. Jixi
liked men to watch her weaving which she did without ceasing,
either under the scorching sun or in the silvery moonlight, until
she fell asleep beside the shining net which encircled her with
the aura of a beautiful mermaid.

Jixi stretched her aged fingers to touch the net and cursed in a
low voice. She then examined the potatoes to see if they were
ready before she put the kettle on the stove to make tea. When
she finished eating and drinking in this dawdling way, dawn was
slowly breaking. Through the translucent window pane, the
Shichuan River could be seen radiating a darkish sheen. Jixi's
house was situated by the river. The opposite bank was covered
with a stretch of woods. Certainly there were no birds to be seen
flying at this time. Jixi looked at the sky for a while. Feeling a
little sleepy, she murmured indistinctly and threw herself on the
kang for a nap. She fell sound asleep and didn't wake up until

disturbed by someone knocking vehemently at her door. The visitor was Hu Hui's grandson Hu Dao, who held two packets of tea and dried dates out to the old lady. He must have left home in a hurry for he was not wearing his cotton-padded hat. His hair was whitened by a thick layer of snow as if he was carrying a flour cake on his head; his two ears were frozen the colour of a ripe haw. He said in a dejected tone, "Aunt Jixi, how should I deal with the matter? The little creature chooses the wrong time to come into this world. Ailian says she feels not quite right; she is going to give birth today. Oh, and the tear fish are coming, how should I deal with the situation? It's not the right time..."

Jixi put the tea and dates on the top of the closet and glanced at this man all in a fluster. Men were always in this state the first time they became a father. Jixi enjoyed watching the scene.

"If she hasn't given birth when the tear fish come, Aunt Jixi, you go to the river to catch them. It's really not the right time, it's about two weeks premature. Why does the little creature want to compete with the fish?..." Hu Dao repeated again and again, standing at the door with his hands at his sides, all the time looking out of the window. What was there? Snow, only snow.

In Ahjia Village, people believed that if a family couldn't catch at least one tear fish when they came, disaster would befall its members. Nobody had suffered any disaster of course, because each family would catch many fish this time each year. Different from other species of fish, tear fish were always found to be alive when caught in a net. About half a kilogramme in weight, small and exquisite, the bluish fish would be put into wooden basins full of water and set free the next morning. Once again in water, the sobbing sounds they emitted would cease. Lucky are those that have the chance to see this rare fish.

Jixi told Hu Dao to go home and prepare a kettle of hot water. She ate a potato and drank a cup of hot tea. Then she put the fishing implements in order, banked up the fire in the stove and put on her silvery grey scarf before going out of the door.

Ahjia Village seemed ever smaller in the swirl of flying snowflakes, with its one hundred or so houses each like a date preserved in white sugar. Jixi shot a glance at the Shichuan River, which appeared emaciated under the winter's first snow. She seemed to sense a subtle trembling of the water as signalling the coming of the tear fish. She remembered Hu Dao's grandfather Hu Hui, who had fallen victim to a black bear at the age of seventy and was buried in the pine woods on the opposite bank. As a young man Hu Hui excelled at riding and shooting and was among the most experienced catchers of tortoises. Though of average size and plain looks, he was the idol in the hearts of Ahjia girls. The young Jixi had been a capable girl, who caught fish, did embroidery, sewing and brewed wine. Hu Hui used to come to her house to smoke a cigarette. Her wooden hut had been set up with his help. The young Jixi had imagined, had been sure, that she would become his wife, but contrary to her wish, he asked for the hand of Caizhu, a homely, but incapable girl. It happened that on the wedding day Jixi was washing fish by the river. When she saw the foolish bridegroom coming near, wearing a red flower on his breast and followed by a procession of men and women on their way to meet the bride, she tossed a whole wooden basin of stinking water brimming with fish scales on his head, laughing delightedly while doing so. Hu Hui beamed an apologetic smile at Jixi and, drenched and smelly, continued on to meet his bride. Jixi took up a fish and swallowed mouthfuls of meat, tears streaming down her face.

Years later, Hu Hui told her the reason why he didn't marry her on the day of catching tear fish. "You're too capable," he said. "You're able to do everything, even to carry a family's burden alone. A man will loose his ability and confidence in life under your roof."

Jixi said desperately, "Is it a fault to be capable?"

According to Jixi, if a woman couldn't catch fish, pickle vegetables and fish, brew wine, or did nothing more than have babies, she couldn't be counted as a lovable woman. This attitude had led to the tragedy in her life. All the men in Ahjia Village appreciated her, liked to drink her wine and tea, to smoke her tobacco leaves and watch the lovely expression of her face and her unusual white teeth when she ate raw fish. However, no man married her. The Shichuan River flowed forward day and night as Jixi became older and older, day by day, while the trees on both banks grew more and more luxuriant.

When Jixi reached middle age, she was particularly fond of singing. She sang when scaling fish on the bank of the river; when going to the mountains to collect mushrooms in autumn; when drying vegetables on the roof of her wooden house; and when she fed her chickens at dusk. Her songs, like cooking smoke, wafted to every corner of the village, stabbing men to the heart as painful and agonising as the sobs of the tear fish. Each time they heard Jixi sing a song they would come to her house for a smoke of tobacco and call her name affectionately time and again, and that would bring an end to Jixi's singing. She would neatly pulverise tobacco leaves, polish the pipes to a bright shine in which all the fine texture of their bronze bowls and wooden hands was revealed. She liked to hear men call her "Jixi", the sound making her more lovely and gentler than ever. But after having smoked her tobacco leaves those men would get up from the *kang*, slip on their shoes and go home. What was left to Jixi was a courtyard of motley tree shadows under the moonlight. Jixi didn't sing after her fortieth birthday. She silently and bravely welcomed the first white hair on her head and started to frequent specific households to acquire the skills of midwifery. How she envied those women for that happy and painful moment of childbirth!

In all her time as a midwife, Jixi had never delivered a child the day the tear fish arrived. Never had she come close to encountering such a thing. On the way to the Hus', she prayed that the child be born before dusk so that she could join the crowd on the bank. Then she found it ridiculous to pray to God amidst flying snowflakes when only a moment ago she had cursed this god in vain.

Hu Dao's wife lay stretched out on the *kang* and beads of sweat rose on her head from the pain of her labour. When she saw Jixi coming in, tears seemed to well up in her eyes. Jixi washed her hands while enquiring how long the pain had lasted and how the woman felt. Hu Dao ran about the room frantically, now kicking over a wooden basin and spilling water everywhere; now over an iron rod tilting against the wall in the corner. "You go and prepare your fishing tools," said Jixi tolerably. "Don't you make a mess here."

"I've already arranged everything."

"What about the firewood?"

"It's ready," said Hu Dao obsequiously.

"The fishing net must be a number three size," she added.

"I have it ready," said Hu Dao in confusion. He was making tea but knocked over the tea caddy, which fell on the ground with clanking noise that made his prostrate wife convulse.

"If you're so capable," Jixi said in an intimidating tone, "how about you come here and deliver your own son?"

At these words, the colour drained from Hu Dao's face. "Aunt Jixi, how can I deliver a child? How can I?"

"In the same way you installed it in the first place," she joked. Only then did Hu Dao realise that his presence added to the nervousness of his wife, so he left in a flurry but fell over the threshold. He groaned, an image both ridiculous and lovable.

On the northern wall of the sitting room hung a portrait of Hu Hui in his youth. He was wearing a black felt hat and a long tobacco pipe dangled from his lips, his face wreathed in smiles.

The first time Jixi saw this picture, she rocked with laughter, "You look really funny, like a monkey. What a terrible image for the painter to present! How dare he?"

"Someday, when I die you won't feel it's funny," said Hu Hui.

He was right. Now when Jixi looked at it, she felt sadness rising in heart.

Two hours had passed but there was no sign that the woman would soon give birth. It was already afternoon. Jixi was becoming upset. If the situation went on like this, she would be late for the arrival of the tear fish. She looked out of the window and saw many people walking in the direction of the river. Some of them had already carried firewood there. Dogs were jumping and running joyously in the snow.

Hu Dao was covering the pig pen with dry grass in the court-

yard, and bits of grass were blown by the wind into the sky,
which danced in mid-air like a shoal of small fish swimming in
water. This scene made Jixi remember that particularly unfor-
gettable day. Fifty years ago, Jixi was stacking dry grass in her
courtyard. She put the grass on the hay stack with the shining
silvery fork. Her jet-black hair was peppered with bits of grass
which sent out a fragrant aroma. The autumn dusk added a feeling of heaviness to the foliage falling in the woods while the
faint frost left fresh tear-like stains on the window panes. When
the setting sun fell into the exuberant woods on the opposite
bank, Jixi saw Hu Hui coming in her direction from the upper
reaches of the Shichuan River. From where she stood, he
looked like an ant wriggling his way towards her; as he moved
nearer he resembled a clumsy frog; right before her he was
transformed into a lovable dog which was wagging his tail.

When Jixi told him the three images she had imagined for
him, Hu Hui roared with laughter, the expression on his face a
beam of satisfaction. He threw a small fish to her and watched
her eat it up bit by bit. Jixi went to prepare tea and food for
him. Then in the dim light of the room, he suddenly held her in
his arms and put his lips on hers. He smelt an aroma particular
to the Shichuan River in her mouth and inhaled mouthfuls for a
long time.

"What did I look like coming from the distance?" He bit at
her lips.

"Like an ant," she replied, panting.

"What about nearer to you?" He held her tighter.

"A frog," she whispered.

"Right before you?" He again bit at her lips.

"A dog with his tail wagging," she said, her body shaking as bits of dry grass dropped from her hair into her neck, which was unbearably itchy.

"And on your body when my face is close to yours?" He carried her onto the *kang* and carefully pulled her clothes from the bottom up.

She didn't utter a sound, for she didn't know what he was like then. As he poured out his deep affection for her in this powerful way the wriggling Jixi suddenly groaned, "You resemble a tiger this moment."

The water in the kettle on the stove was boiling, the steam continuously puffing, puffing, and pushing up the lid. Jixi paid no attention to it and let the kettle sing on. When they eventually parted, both perspiring, the whole kettle of water had evapourated into white steam, leaving the room cosy and warm.

The memorable evening reassured her that Hu Hui was to marry her, and that her future would be to make tea and cook for him, to give birth to his sons and do everything he liked. But he married another woman. When she tossed the fishy water right on him on his wedding day, she felt the sun was so pale and cold and cruel. From that day on, she would not allow Hu Hui to enter into her house. She was willing to give her tobacco and tea to any man but him. When he died, all the villagers attended the funeral except her. She stood behind the window in her house, looking out at the Shichuan River which flowed forward day and night. She seemed to hear the puffs of boiling water pushing against the kettle lid.

The woman on the *kang* groaned again, and the moans forced Jixi to move away from Hu Hui's portrait. "You really look like a funny monkey," she muttered, and habitually added a curse to God.

"Am I going to die, Aunt Jixi?" The woman stretched her wet hand out of the blanket.

"All women at their first childbirth would think of death, but none of them die. You have me here, you won't die," Jixi comforted her while wiping the sweat away from her forehead with a towel. "What do you want, a son or a daughter?"

"Either as long as it's healthy," the woman beamed a tired smile.

"Now you're thinking this way," said Jixi, sitting on the edge of the bed. "But as soon as the child is born, you will be hard on it. Look at your belly, you are likely to give birth to twins."

The woman was terrified. "It's already going to be hard e-nough to give birth to one child, and now two!"

Jixi said, "Women are too delicate. They take a whole day to give birth to one child and they groan the whole time. Look at dogs and cats. They usually give birth to three or five siblings at a time with no one waiting on them. Cats even have to pick up cotton to make a nest by themselves before giving birth. Surely they feel pain too, but they are not as fragile as women."

Her words silenced the woman for a moment. But before long the will of the mother-to-be softened like a block of ice under the sun. She groaned again and cursed, "Are you dead, Hu Dao? You won't care after you have done evil. Hu Dao, why don't you come here to give birth by yourself? You seek only gratification..."

Jixi laughed inwardly.

It was getting dark. Hu Dao had already finished his work and was now bundling up the dry firewood that was to be used at night on the river bank. The snow that had been falling began to ease off. At a careless glance, it even appeared to have stopped.

Yet deep snow had already accumulated on the ground. It formed a spectacular sight on the Korean pine fence: each red railing was crowned with a white flower of snow, the contrast of colours suggestive of gentleness and passion all rolled into one.

As night set in, Jixi felt an ache in her heart. She heard dogs in the village bark joyously and saw people set up bonfires beside the river. The expectant mother had calmed down once more. As she had sweated hard, the reed mat under her body had become soaked. Jixi lit a candle. The woman beamed an apologetic smile to her and said, "Aunt Jixi, please go catch the tear fish. Without you being there, the villagers will find it less interesting."

It was true. Each year at this season, Jixi could catch dozens or even one hundred tear fish, so active that when they were put into the wood basin they commanded attention of all the villagers, especially children, who would mischievously dive their hands into the basin, grasp the tail or head of a fish and churn the whole basin up a chaotic frenzy. Their parents would come over and exhort them; "Be careful! Don't you hurt their scales!"

Jixi said, "If I go, who will help you deliver the child?"

"I'll do it myself," said the woman. "Tell me how to cut off the umbilical cord. Tell Hu Dao to go too. I'm all right to stay at home alone."

"See how capable you can be!" Jixi rebuked her in an affectionate tone.

The woman moved her leg. Then she asked, "If one of the villagers doesn't catch a fish, will he die?"

"Who knows, it's merely a legend," answered Jixi. "Besides, it never happens that a family doesn't catch at least one tear fish."

"When I was a little girl," the woman said in a thin voice, "I always asked my parents: why do the tear fish cry? Why do they have blue scales? Why do they come only after the first snow? They couldn't answer my questions. Aunt Jixi, can you tell me?"

"How could I know?" murmured Jixi, her hands hanging silently down at her sides. "You might go and ask the river. She might know."

Another fit of pain stabbed the woman, and she began to groan again.

It was all dark now. The bonfires on the bank of the river shone brightly. When faint sobs were heard in the flowing water, fishermen became busy throwing the silvery nets out into the river, loath to lose one minute. Their wives had already filled their basins with water. Now, heads wrapped with grey or blue scarves, they walked here and there on the bank. Snow-shrouded trees covered the mountains on the opposite bank. A marvellous moon rose high up in the sky, its cool and clear light shining over the river, the bonfires, the wood basins and the fishermen's sunburnt faces. Now the sad sobs floating downstream from the upper reaches were becoming louder and louder.

Wuwuu... wuwu... wuwuwu...

As if thousands of small boats had come down from the upper reaches, as if all the falling foliage on earth had swarmed into the river, and as if all the most sentimental tunes had fused into one melody, the Shichuan River resounded with tragic and desperate sobs, cloaking the people of Ahjia Village in an almost religious atmosphere. The first tear fish that was caught wagged its tail slightly while tears streamed down its face. The man's wife quickly put it into a basin and began her comforting, "There, there, don't cry; there, there, don't cry..." The orange fire illuminated her bronze-coloured complexion and her dark blue scarf.

Wuwuwu... wuwuwuwuwu... wuwuwu...

Night was getting deeper. As Hu Dao had already caught seven tear fish he ran back home to see his wife. The poor woman lay with her wide-open eyes fixed on the ceiling, blank her gaze, hopeless and desperate.

"Does the little creature want to come out after the tear fish season finishes?" thought Jixi to herself.

"Aunt Jixi, let me stay here. You go and make your catch. I've already got seven," said Hu Dao.

"What's the use of your waiting here? You aren't able to deliver a child."

"If she gives birth, I will fetch you. Perhaps..." Hu Dao hesitated for a moment before saying, "Perhaps she'll give birth tomorrow."

"Certainly not. She is to give birth before midnight," Jixi said.

Jixi drank a cup of tea, and that refreshed her. She lit a second candle to replace the first and started to relate some funny mistakes she had made when she was young. The woman listened carefully and laughed. Jixi felt somewhat relieved as she saw the woman distracted from her burden.

About eleven at night, the woman again was drowned in painful contractions. At first she groaned in a low voice but finally burst out shouting. The sight of Hu Dao coming in and out of the room seemed to be the root of her suffering. She almost roared with rage. Jixi asked Hu Dao to light another candle and she held it beside the woman. Finally, Jixi saw a baby's head appear like a ripe apple. Her heart brimmed with happiness. She encouraged, "Try again, it's coming. Don't be afraid; push! I'm already late for the tear fish."

The scarlet fruit finally emerged from its mother's womb, its lively crying, as well as a fragrant aroma, filling the air.

"Oh, little girl, you've got a loud voice. Certainly you will enjoy eating raw fish when you grow up," Jixi said, then calmly waited for the coming of the second child. Ten minutes passed and then another ten. The woman breathed heavily and yelled. At the shout, a baby rushed out of her body and cried in an unusually loud voice. It was a healthy boy!

"Hu Dao, Hu Dao," shouted Jixi, "you're lucky to have twins, a boy and a girl!"

Hu Dao was so excited he flitted around like a busy bee. He looked at his wife who was now calming down, with gratitude, as she lay more comfortably on the wet reed mat now dotted with drops of blood. She felt happy that she had successfully finished the task of giving birth to twins for the Hu family.

"Aunt Jixi," said the woman in a weak voice, "I hope it is not too late for you to go to the Shichuan River."

Jixi washed her bloody hands clean and had a cup of tea before she wrapped her scarf around her head and walked out of the room. Passing by the sitting room, she instinctively turned her head in the direction of the ridiculous portrait of Hu Hui, but to her great surprise, there was nothing there except a wooden bottle gourd and two wooden shuttles. Could it be that she had seen the spirit of Hu Hui? The air in the courtyard was refreshing and she breathed more comfortably, feeling as if she had been given an additional lung. Hu Dao was burning some-

thing, the fire jumped actively, illuminating the whole courtyard.

"What are you burning?" asked Jixi curiously.

"My grandfather's portrait. When he was alive, he told us
that if he could not see his great-grandson with his own eyes,
then let his portrait do it, and that after his great-grandson was
born, there was no need for his portrait to hang on the wall."

Jixi looked at the dying fire, thinking mournfully, "Hu Hui,
you really got to see your great-grandson. But sadly it is not Jixi
who was responsible for carrying on the Hu family line."

Hu Dao continued, "My grandfather said that a man could only be responsible for his sons and grandsons; that great-grand-
sons would regard him as a monster. So he said when his great-
grandson was born his portrait should be destroyed so that no
man might remember him."

The portrait shrank bit by bit and at last vanished.

Tears streamed down her face as she listened to the faint sobs
rising from the Shichuan River. She was no longer able to eat
raw fish, whose scales had made such carefree sounds between
her teeth before. Most of her teeth had dropped out, and her
gums, which used to be so appealingly red, were now dark purple like a dilapidated wall that suffered from smoke erosion day
and night. Her hair was sparse and white, like a cluster of deserted dry grass in winter.

She allowed her tears to fall continuously on her way back
home. Putting the net on her old shoulder she walked toward the
river with difficulty, carrying the wooden basin in one hand.
The bonfires on the bank were still bright, illuminating the snow
on the opposite bank in a golden yellow light. Women stood by
their basins in which tear fish were swimming in a leisurely man-

ner, and looked at Jixi. None of the sad sounds particular to the Shichuan River came out of the water; the river was tranquil. Jixi threw out her net into the river and with difficulty, filled the basin with water. Afterwards, she waited blankly for the coming of tear fish. She heard the footsteps of people coming and going behind her, and recalled the basin of fishy water that she had thrown at Hu Hui. In those days she was so strong that she could do anything she liked. One particularly sad thing was that now she was so old that she had not much strength left in her body. Feeling a bit cold she pulled down a corner of her scarf over her chest.

She started hauling her net, which skimmed over the water lightly. The lightness weighed heavily upon her heart. As expected, the net was empty. But this didn't discourage her. There must be one tear fish within range of her net. She refused to believe that she would leave for home empty-handed. When the eastern sky began to display the first sign of dawn, Jixi hauled in her net for the second time. She pulled it carefully. It was heavy. Her legs trembled but the thought of the beautiful blue fish jumping in the net kept her mind on what she was doing. When the ends of the net appeared, it suddenly dawned on her that she caught nothing again. She cursed and sat down on the bank. One thing perplexed her: why did it feel so heavy when there was nothing in the net? Finally she realised: she was getting old and her strength was failing her.

The dawn rose gradually. The bonfires died out silently; the mountains on the opposite bank were becoming clearly visible. Many fishermen began to return the tear fish they had caught back to the river. Jixi heard the splashing of water, the sound of the tear fish reentering the river. All the fish swam quickly following the flow of water down to the lower reaches of the river. Jixi imagined she saw their blue backs, red fins, and their slightly swaying tails. They come quickly and go away quickly too, thought Jixi. They are really incredible. So small compared with man, yet they can swim the whole length of the Shichuan River year after year. People can only find a place on the bank, live there and grow old till death takes them away. Then they are buried on the bank, their tombs facing the river so that they can continue to listen to the gurgling water.

She felt like singing though her voice was already coarse at this advanced age. But at this moment, she found herself unable to utter a sound. The empty net was spread on the bank, enjoying the soft caress of morning's first sunshine, the mesh now possessed of a soft sheen.

The fishermen went home one after another after they freed the tear fish, followed by their wives carrying the wooden basins and fishing nets, then children and dogs, leaving footprints in the warm ashes of the bonfires. Jixi stood up slowly and collected up her net. The bank was deserted. She moved with difficulty towards her basin. She received the greatest shock when she saw a dozen or so beautiful blue tear fish swimming contentedly in her basin. They moved this way and that in such a carefree way! Tears rolled down her face. She looked up at those distant shadows of the fishermen and their wives and children on their way back to the village, above whose heads a sliver of scarlet red cloud had appeared on the horizon, soaking Ahjia Village in rays of peace and warmth. Jixi quivered and felt like saying something in praise of God's creation, but no words came out of her mouth except her habitual curse.

She collected all her strength and dragged the wooden basin to the water. Kneeling down and panting heavily, she stretched her emaciated hands down to pluck the fish from the basin. One by one, she put them back into the river, which, being the last to return to whence they had come, swam quickly through the water the moment they dived into the current.

Translated by Chen Haiyan

A Flock in the Wilderness

1. Decision

YU Wei drove the jeep to the sandy bank. A murky grey river appeared before us like an old faded picture.

"Just look, there's a fishing boat over there," Yu Wei cried out.

Sure enough, a boat was rowing steadily forward in the direction Yu Wei was pointing. On the boat were two men in dull-coloured clothes, who appeared like figures in a silent film from a bygone age.

"They really are like the two characters in *The Sunrise*," I blurted out.

"You mean the drama by Cao Yu?" Yu Wei asked indifferently.

"No, I mean an American film," I answered distractedly. "It's about a man and a woman. They often meet by a river. The woman rows a boat wearing a large floppy straw hat." I chattered interminably: "Silent film is the best kind for love stories. And black-white ones are even better."

"Doctrine of 'back to the old ways'." Yu Wei unconsciously pressed the horn.

The boat was approaching us. The two men began busily to haul in the net which was the same colour as the water in the river and looked grey and old. No glittering fish scales appeared; their net was empty.

"They don't seem to have caught anything," I sighed.

"How could they catch fish in a season like this?" said Yu Wei.

It was late autumn. All the poplar trees had become leafless, and the small willows along the riverside were no longer delicate and bright. Although the first snow had not yet come, the white frost on the withered yellow leaves lying on the ground and the greyish sky indicated a snowstorm in the offing.

The little boat carrying the empty net turned slowly back in the direction from which it had come. The rower gazed around at the stern, while the other man huddled at the bows looking cold. The boat gradually disappeared into the distance.

Yu Wei and I fell silent. As we turned our gaze to the other side of the river, a shabby dredger came in sight. A tent was set up on the river bank where a few people were digging sands. They too were dressed in drab clothing. After a gust of wind I noticed the surface of the water ripple as though the entire river was shaking. I threw open the door of the jeep and walked toward a tract of reeds on the left side. The wind blew up strands of my hair. I watched the soughing reeds dancing in the wind, which ran on, over pools of foul water on the blackish silt left over from floods. Unable to go deeper into the reeds, I could only gaze at them from above the silt.

The outline of Bafangtai Village could be seen lying behind the tract of reeds. This village was home to someone about whom I had made a decision.

I walked back to the jeep rubbing my hands that were by now frozen red.

"Decided?" Yu Wei turned to me.

"Let's go!" I said.

Yu Wei started the engine but the wheels sank into the sand. He stepped on the gas, and the spinning wheels sent puffs of sand flying onto the glass of the rear window, producing a great din. The jeep jolted a few times before humming its way over the beach like a proud old man, forward to the solid black dirt road. Yu Wei drove so slowly I could see in detail the dry cakes of cow dung and balls of horse droppings, withered branches and grass on the road. It was getting late. After a day of cold, the sun unexpectedly revealed a store of energy surreptitiously acquired during the day, and turned fiery red before it set itself down.

The road ahead forked into a broad fairway which led back to the city and a narrow, uneven dust track which ran to Bafangtai Village. "Which road should we take?" Yu Wei asked in a low voice. I pointed to the broad one.

Yu Wei stopped the jeep but did not cut the engine, so I could still feel the vehicle shaking lightly like a man in a rage.

"Why?" Yu Wei asked impatiently. "You do this every time. You always sneak away at the critical moment. What are you afraid of? If we don't go there today, the child will never be ours."

"He's not our child anyway," I retorted bitterly. "I've suffered enough. Let's get divorced. That's the best way out. It benefits both of us. And we will. . ."

"Still talking the same old nonsense!" Yu Wei pressed the horn angrily, which frightened a crow out of a nearby withered old tree.

"We can give up the child," Yu Wei's voice softened. "But we can't get a divorce."

"But you want to have a child. You're already forty." I could not help sobbing loud. "I'm incapable. I can't figure out how to be the mother of a child who's a complete stranger to me."

"Well" Yu Wei sighed. "Don't cry anymore. I'll never mention it again." He stretched out his hand to caress my hair. "I know you are capable. You'll bear me many children, like a flock of sheep."

"But what if I can't bear you any children?" I said.

"We'll live on just as well." Yu Wei forced a smile. "We'll be more deeply attached to each other than other couples." He tried to enliven the atmosphere. "And we can still go for drives together on Sundays. That won't be bad at all."

"There's a very simple solution to the problem." I stopped sobbing. "All you need to do is to find another woman."

"You always bring that nonsense up. How many times do I have to say it? You're my wife—for life!" Yu Wei lowered his voice: "No prattle anymore. We're not newlyweds. Do I need to pledge my troth again?"

"There's no need to go that far," I mumbled.

"You women are really hard to deal with, always want to be flattered," Yu Wei sighed. "My final word on the subject is that you mustn't mention this nonsense again. Moreover, you mustn't cry anymore. You know I hate to see your tears."

Yu Wei got out of the jeep and stood in the wind for a while. His bushy hair was fluffed up in the wind, and reminded me of the vigorous flames of a stove in winter. When he got back to the jeep, he patted me on the shoulder and said, "OK, let's go back to the city." Then he lowered his voice and added: "I'll never give up on you."

With a jerk the jeep leapt out of a ditch onto the fairway heading for the city. I cast a glance in the direction of Bafangtai Village. The setting sun had become scarlet red and was sinking fast. The dwellings in Bafangtai were still faintly visible. I suddenly felt a strong desire rising within me, and said hurriedly, "Stop, quickly, Yu Wei."

Yu Wei put on the brakes. "What's wrong?"

"Let's go to Bafangtai," I said to him. "I want that child."

Yu Wei stared at me in amazement. After a long while, he said, "Don't force yourself to accept things you don't want."

"It's not things," I retorted. "It's our future child."

"You must think it over more carefully. This isn't something you can change your mind about later." Yu Wei added: "I hate to see you feel sad."

Gazing the magnificent setting sun with fixed eyes, I urged: "Let's go to the village quickly. I seemed to hear that child was calling me."

Yes indeed, I heard the burning voice of the setting sun, a voice of life which was marching on and calling.

2. A Three-Member Family

The labyrinthine layout of Bafangtai Village gave us a lot of trouble. As the jeep ran round along lanes in the village, we discovered that the houses, courtyards, pigpens and henhouses were all of the same style. Even the villagers who walked with lowered head along the dirt road beyond the twig fences wore the same expression on their faces. We stopped our jeep to ask an old man: "How to go to Wang Jicheng's house?" The old man, who was wearing a black, thinly lined jacket, his two hands hidden in his sleeves, had a thin long face and purplish lips. When he opened his mouth to speak he shivered with cold. He pouted his lips toward the place where our jeep parked and said that we were at the right place. When we said our thanks to him, I had the impression that a sad expression suddenly flitted across his eyes.

Yu Wei and I gazed at each other in speechless apprehension, so taken back that we did not know what to say to him. Although we still did not know the exact location of Wang Jicheng's house, our jeep was right there. Yu Wei pulled my hand and encouraged me to enter the courtyard with him.

The first thing that came into view in the courtyard was a small flower nursery below the window in front of the house. Chrysanthemums and poppy vines listlessly twisted together after the frost, and two cinereous hens flicked the earth to and fro in the flower bed. Atop the wall that ran up at the back of the flower bed there were various bundles of vegetable seeds. If this old house should be described as resembling a silent, mysterious Indian, then the bundles of vegetable seeds which swayed gently in the evening breeze were like the feathers fixed aslant in his headdress. On the yellowish sandy ground were droppings from chickens and dogs. But there were no dogs barking there. Perhaps they had deserted their master, following their own diversions elsewhere. Either side of the door were piles of dry grass, shovels and waste paper boxes, while on the lintel over the door were Chinese mugworts and calabashes the colour of paper money browned by exposure to wind and rain; they were the perpetual mementos the family had retained from the Dragon Boat Festival.

Yu Wei pushed the door open. I grasped his hand tightly, my heart beating fast, and my palms perspiring as if we were thieves. It was already dusk, but the light had not yet been turned on in the house. A filthy smell assaulted my nostrils. In the dim light I saw a kitchen range and a few cooking utensils. On the earthen wall were some bamboo strainers and curtains which looked like archaeological finds.

We walked past the kitchen and stood before the door of the inner room. "Is Wang Jicheng in?" Yu Wei asked, his voice quivering. Like me he was nervous too.

There was no reply, but the door was suddenly pushed open. A girl of around five years old emerged, her little lips curled up as she cast an angry glance at us. We guessed she must be Wang Jicheng's daughter. Her eyes brimming with tears, she stared at us for a while before making her way towards us reluctantly.

A tall middle-aged woman, wearing cloth shoes, stood up from an earthen *kang* bed to greet us. Her eyes were red and swollen, but her hair was smooth as if it had just been combed. She spoke with a twang: she must have wept for some time.

Two greasy glasses sat on a low cupboard, the paint of which had peeled off. As the woman turned to take up a thermos flask to pour hot water for us, I caught a clear sight of her delicate back.

"I didn't think you would come today," she said as she poured the water.

"We were delayed by something we had to do on the way," Yu Wei hemmed.

"I knew you were coming when I heard the sound of the engine." The woman turned to hand us the glasses of water. The water was boiling hot, but the look that accompanied it was distinctly cold.

We put the glasses on the windowsill, and spontaneously went to see the child lying at the end of the *kang* bed. There, covered only with a thin, worn-out cotton blanket, the small boy was sleeping soundly. Yu Wei caressed his hair lightly with his palm, looked at him with affection and then touched the boy's nose and lips gently with his fingers. Yu Wei's fatherly love for the boy moved me to tears; he needed to have a child indeed.

"The child is a very light sleeper. If you touch his ears, he will wake up immediately. His ears are very sensitive." The woman sighed slightly. "He's slept for over twenty minutes. He'll wake up soon. He never sleeps for long."

The little girl took the two glasses of hot water from the windowsill and threw the water into a plant pot. The woman snatched her over angrily, slapped her on the back and scolded: "What do you think you're doing? Our guests haven't drunk their water yet. And you've scalded the young plants. Go outside!"

The little girl neither resisted nor cried. She just fixed her angry eyes on us when her mother hit her and uttered not a sound.

Panting, the middle-aged woman switched on the light. In the dim glow a gentle smile appeared on the face of the sleeping baby; perhaps he was dreaming a beautiful dream. He had a small mouth, a little nose, arched eyebrows, slightly sunk eyelids and fair skin—a very pretty baby.

"To be honest, I really don't want to give him up," the woman said suddenly sobbing. "But you see..." she pointed to the little girl who hadn't left the room but stood in a rage to one side. "The eldest child's almost six years old. The second child is a boy, already four years old—he's out with his father today. It's too difficult for us to raise the three of them. We heard you wanted to have a child, and we thought it would be good to give the third to you. With him living with you, our two families will become related."

"Your husband is not at home, can you make the decision yourself?" Yu Wei asked.

"He can't bear to see his child being taken away with his own eyes, so he went out with the second child early this morning. He's been away a whole day, and didn't even come back for lunch."

"What does the baby like to eat?" I asked with great care.

"He's seven months old, and still mainly breast-fed," the woman told me with a worried look on her face. "As you know, we don't have much good food to eat when we are in confinement in the countryside. Millet gruel and a few eggs are considered the best. So I didn't have much milk to give him." She cast a glance at Yu Wei. "Your financial situation is much better. You can feed him with powdered milk and a bit of egg yolk. After he is one year old, you can feed him with gruel." Distractedly she turned to stare at me. "Are you sure you will not bear any children yourself?"

"I'm sterile," I said, embarrassed. "Otherwise, I wouldn't"

"Some sterile women are curable. Are you curable?" The woman asked aggressively.

I shook my head. Yu Wei put his hand over my shoulders affectionately.

"The child was born on March 8, about six o'clock in the evening," the woman began to explain the baby's habits. "He doesn't like to sleep on hot bed. Don't put too many clothes on him. He doesn't like to be frightened and is very timid. Of course all small children are the same. You can see his hair is

not very good, so you must often take him to the barbers in the
future so that his hair will grow better. The second day of the
second month of the lunar calendar is an auspicious day. You'd
best have his hair cut on that day. He loves to suck his fingers,
but don't worry about it. He'll stop after he's one year old."

"What does Wang Jicheng usually do at home?" Yu Wei
asked.

"He's clever with his hands. He can do carpentry. In the
past, after the crops were harvested, he would make trunks,
cupboards, tables and chairs for people who were going to get
married in winter."

"You can rest assured, we'll treat the child well," I told the
woman. "We'll give him a good education."

"You can set your minds at rest, too," the woman said.
"Once you take the child away, we won't go to the city to see
him." Her voice quivered. "I beg you to treat him as your own
flesh and blood. Don't let him feel wronged."

"We promise we'll treat him well," Yu Wei said.

He looked at the little girl who stood in abject silence, with
tears in her eyes. She was wearing a cotton-padded jacket with
small flower patterns against a blue background. The two plaits
on her head looked like sheep's horns but the hair was thin and
yellowish. She had a pointed chin and a pair of extremely large
eyes. Yu Wei fished out five hundred dollars and handed it to
her.

"Uncle gives this money to you," he told her. "You can use it
later for your tuition fees when you go to school." Then he
turned to the woman: "Please let us know if you have any difficulties at home. We'll also be responsible for your eldest child's
tuition fees in the future."

The little girl stepped back to huddle herself in the corner, her two hands behind her, staring at us blankly. Suddenly, she burst out crying: "I want my little brother! I want my little brother!"

Her cry, like the eruption of a volcano, awakened the sleeping baby, who rolled up on the *kang* and began to cry. The woman hurried over to gather him into her arms, and we all rose to look at him. His mouth twitching, he cried on. His pitch-dark round eyes which shone with the light of intelligence were thoroughly wet. When he saw Yu Wei and me, he stopped crying, snuggled up in his mother's arms and looked at us timidly.

"He's a bit shy with strangers, and you'll have some trouble tonight," the woman told us. "It'll be all right after three or four days." The woman lowered her head to give him a kiss on the forehead. "When you kiss him, don't kiss his cheeks. That way will make him slobber."

We nodded.

"Let me feed him once more," the woman said, "so that he can leave on a full stomach." She began to unbutton her jacket, and Yu Wei went hastily away to soothe the little girl who stood by, mopping off the tears from her cheeks. A loose breast hung out. Its nipple was dark brown instead of purplish red. The baby caught it and began to suck. It became very quiet in the room. Under the light the woman pressed her breasts hard wanting to squeeze all the milk out for her son, while the baby's cheeks bulged and he drank naively with his eyes fixed at his mother's face. The sound of his sucking was so touching, I almost lost the strength to take him away from his mother. When his feed was over, the woman kissed the baby's forehead once again before she put him on the *kang*, wrapped him with a cotton blanket and handed him over to me shakily. I was so nervous, I felt almost suffocated, and pantingly took the baby in my arms. The baby started crying as soon as I took hold of him and struggled to stretch out his little hands to grasp his mother.

"Please leave quickly," the woman said, tears streaming down her cheeks.

Yu Wei and I started to walk out, but before we reached the door, the little girl flung herself at me and grabbed my leg, even gripping it with her teeth. Fortunately, I was wearing long woollen underwear and did not feel much pain. The woman moved forward to take the little girl back. Scarcely had we walked out of the door, when a profound wailing burst out in the house.

We hastily got into the jeep. Yu Wei started the engine, but the baby went on crying. My face was running with stream of sweat, I did not know what to do and burst out crying myself.

The blood-red setting sun had sunk, dusk had enveloped Bafangtai Village. Yu Wei turned on the headlights and drove toward the outskirts of the village. There were no pedestrians to be seen on the way. Once out of the village, the road widened and the boundless wilderness lay undulating before us. The little baby gradually stopped crying to fix his surprised eyes at the road ahead. My mind slowly calmed down, and tears ceased to flow down my cheeks, too. Yu Wei turned to cast a smiling glance at me, saying, "It's really a lovely boy."

"That's your papa," I said to the baby.

His eyes fixed at the road ahead, Yu Wei drove very fast. Perhaps he wished to leave Bafangtai as soon as possible. I removed the baby's hands from the cotton blanket wrapper, fished out a pen from my pocket and gave it to him to play with. Gripping the pen in hand, the baby began to play with it merrily. All of a sudden, a current of warmth ran through me; we had a child that belonged to us at long last, our family was no longer the two of us but a three-some.

The three members of our family were running fast on the country road, leaving Bafangtai far behind.

3. Luwei's World

Yu Wei and I did not sleep a wink the night the baby arrived in our home. He cried for half the night until he had exhausted himself and finally succumbed to sleep after drinking half a bottle of milk. Lying on the bed, Yu Wei and I discussed what kind of nurse we would hire for the baby. I preferred a young one because young girls were dexterous and could play with the child and, more importantly, could speak standard Chinese. But Yu Wei favoured hiring a healthy elder woman, as elder women had experience of, and patience in, looking after children. Finally Yu Wei's opinion got the upper hand. It was already past midnight when the matter was finally settled. Then we began to discuss what name we should give to the child. Yu Wei said that it did not follow the fashion for a child to be named after the father, so it was better for the baby to take my family name. "Call him Bai Luwei," I blurted out quickly. Yu Wei agreed with my suggestion saying the name was very romantic and he only hoped the baby would not become too romantic when he grew up. After that we came to the subject of how to register the child, and how to buy a pushcart, toys and clothes for him. We did not stop until dawn was breaking and we became too tired to go on. Yu Wei held me in his arms and said in a low voice to my ear, "Seems we must cancel one activity in our routine programme of holiday events. Look, how tired you are now!"

"Aren't you also too tired for that?" I countered flirtatiously. He smiled sheepishly in tacit agreement. Before we had slept very long, we were woken by the baby's crying. He had kicked away his cotton blanket leaving his backside bare, and his face and neck were all flush from crying. In a muddle I hurriedly picked him up and nursed him in my arms. Yu Wei patted the little cotton mattress the baby had slept on with his hand and said with a worried frown, "It's wet through."

Little Luwei, who had received his name but a brief while ago, did not stop crying no matter how hard I tried to coax him. Yu Wei got so worried he tweaked Luwei's ears, scratched his cheeks and made a wry face toward him. In the past when I got annoyed, he had used that trick to coax me and succeeded each time. But little Luwei did not take to it at all. The more he looked at the wry face, the harder he cried. Yu Wei pulled a long face and took down everything from the cupboard in an attempt to please him, but to no avail. He cried on and on till a heart-shaped alarm clock was shown to him. He sobbingly reached his little hand out and ceased crying. We hastily changed mattress and made a bottle of milk for him. After playing with the alarm clock for a while and drinking the milk he went to sleep peacefully. Only then did we heave a sigh of relief. Day had already broken. I fried two eggs, sliced a few pieces of bread and prepared two cups of warm milk. Sitting in front of our breakfast listlessly, we had no appetite. Yu Wei's eyes were blood shot. In a downcast mood, I asked myself if we didn't make a serious mistake.

"Don't worry. Things will get better in a few days," Yu Wei

said to comfort me. "We just need a bit of time to get to know each other."

"Perhaps you're right," I said rashly, feeling a big wronged. "When I took a little dog home when I was a child, even that barked for a good few days!"

Yu Wei pouted his lips and laughed. "Just think what you've just compared him to...."

I could not help laughing too. "Anyway, we must find a nurse for the child as soon as possible."

"We'd better let the child have some time to get to know us first," Yu Wei suggested. "We're to be his parents. If the nurse comes, the child might take her as his dear one, not us. Do you understand what I mean?"

"Of course," I agreed. "It also takes time to find a nurse."

Previously, after Yu Wei had gone to work I would be left behind quietly in my studio to paint. When I became tired, I listened to music, did some reading, or drank tea. But now it was different. Just as I had finished tidying up the house, and before I even had time to wash my hands, Luwei woke up. He woke himself up crying. I rushed over to pick him up, comforting him with a rocking motion of my arms, singing children's songs for him. But all my efforts were in vain. Luwei wrestled in my arms, and I did not know how to deal with him. Neither did I have any idea why he was crying. Did he want milk, to play with a toy, or to pee? Just as I approached the heights of bewilderment, he suddenly ceased crying, shrugged his shoulders, opened his eyes wide and shuddered. A serious look came up his face. I was contemplating what to do next when, all of a sudden, a warm liquid thing landed in the hand that was supporting his buttocks followed by an offensive smell. It threw me in a flurry, and I did not think to just hold him out to let him empty the bowels. My brain became totally numb, and ceased to function at that moment. So it was my mistake to let my hand remain there. When he finished his task my hand looked as if it had been daubed with a thick layer of golden yellow mud. I got some toilet paper to clean my hand first and then his buttocks, after which I warmed some water to give him a bath. When I put his naked body into the warm water in the bathtub he started a fit of giggles. This was the first time he laughed with his new mother.

A week went by. Luwei had quietened down. He no longer cried at night. Yu Wei had bought a big pile of toys from the children's shop for him. Our baby had all he wanted and began to show an affection for me. When I stretched out my arms to carry him, he would greet me with out-spread hands. After having eaten and drunk his fill, he would try to speak out some thought in a squeaky voice, while he tirelessly played with his toys. One afternoon, after he had drunk his milk, he crawled to and fro in his cot. Wearing a pair of blue wool trousers, he smiled a sweet hearty smile at me whenever he caught sight of me. A sudden inspiration arose in me, and I hastily set up my easel, sat down by his side and painted a picture of him which I titled *The Afternoon Luwei in His Cot*. I painted the light with great care so that the picture was neither too dark nor too pale, just like the sheen on spring water in the morning sun. Out of curiosity, Luwei crawled forward several times to the edge of the cot and held the rail to watch me painting. When I smiled at him, he responded by tapping the rail of the cot with his little hands noisily.

The first thing Yu Wei did when he came back in the evening

was to take up the child from the cot to the window to show him the running cars, pedestrians and bill-boards on the street. Luwei emitting a "wa, wa" sound as if he understood everything. When Yu Wei turned round he discovered my painting entitled *The Afternoon Luwei in His Cot* I had put in the corner of the room, and cried out: "What a wonderful painting!"

I popped my head out from the kitchen and said proudly, "Of course, it is."

"A painting full of warmth," Yu Wei commented. "It's not like the paintings you made before, which were full of cold and terror. All I saw in those was desolate scenery or exaggerated, deformed figures. But this painting has none of those great patches of light grey or dark brown. It looks very smooth and bright. The blue colour and the light are all very convincing."

"The credit must go to Luwei," I exclaimed.

"Yes, the credit must go to our son." Yu Wei gave a forceful kiss at the child's forehead.

A fortnight later, after Luwei had established his affection for us, the nurse came. She was a fifty-seven-year-old woman, fair-skinned, refined and courteous, with a pair of deep-set eyes. She had worked as a university teacher before she retired. Her family name was Lin, so I called her Auntie Lin. During the first few days I felt worried about her, fearing that she would not endure the hardships as to clean the child's buttocks or hold him out to let him urinate. But facts proved that all my worries were unnecessary. She not only worked hard but also was very efficient, and was not one for mindless chatter. Luwei became very fond of her. From chatting with her I came to know that her husband had passed away and her only daughter resided faraway in America. She lived all by herself and felt very lonely at home, so she went out to find some job to occupy the time.

"Why did you have the idea of being a nurse?" I asked her without mincing the words.

"I heard the child's mother was Bai Xufei," she said honestly. "The year before last I saw your exhibition and was deeply impressed by one painting called *Running Spring Water on the Earth*."

"You like paintings?" I was surprised.

"Both my deceased husband and myself liked paintings," she said. "In my sparetime I liked to do some Chinese ink and wash myself. I loved to paint things like bamboo, calabash, peonies, chrysanthemums, horses and orchids." When she talked about the past her eyes shone with an especially soft light. "But I was not particularly interested in ink and wash. I liked oils most."

"Did you try your hand at that?" I asked.

She smiled and lightly put the baby who was huddling up to sleep in her arms to the cot. "I did paint a few oils, but they weren't very good. You know, I didn't receive any professional training. When I began to use the paint for the first time, I really didn't know where to start."

"But you painted anyway," I said, both surprised and excited. "When you come next time why don't you bring some to show me."

"In fact I've brought some with me today," she said a bit timidly. "But I didn't dare to take them out to show you."

It was dusk. In the room only Luwei's gentle snoring could be heard. Sitting in my studio I was waiting for Auntie Lin to take her paintings for me with the same uneasy state of mind as that when I went to Bafangtai to get the baby. Time ticked past second by second. With high expectations, I felt each of the ticks as a metallic sound pleasing to the ear. Finally, Auntie Lin carried her paintings to my studio and said pantingly to me, "These four paintings are all I have. If you're disappointed looking at the first one, please don't feel obliged to look at the others."

I sat in a rattan chair by the window, while Auntie Lin stood at about a metre from the door. We were five or six metres apart. I asked her to move closer to me as though I were some kind of expert myself. Obediently she took a few steps nearer. When I saw her face was softly tinted with the evening glow coming in through the window, I said eagerly, "The light's right. Let's take a look."

She bent to put the paintings on the floor, then picked up the one on the top and unrolled it slowly toward me. In order not to let the painting quiver, she held her breath and kept as stiff as a statue.

I was astonished: a golden dancing girl was spinning before me. I could not see her eyes as her head was rather small. Her arms were spread out, and her long and heavy skirt almost dominated the picture. From her slightly tilted head and fiery skirt, I could sense that she was dancing in the prime of life, ardent, proud and yet somewhat gloomy.

"The second painting, please," I said hurriedly.

Here was the same golden dancing girl who, standing before the counter in a bar, holding a glass and lightly sipping wine. A young waiter wearing a tie was gaping at her attentively, all against violet flowers dotted at the background.

In the third painting the dancing girl had turned pale, sat wearily gazing at her hands in front of a gate. Hers were golden, delicate hands. A waiter holding a plate and a smoker with a big belly were frozen in the background.

The dancing girl in the fourth painting was seated high at a counter in a bar, with one foot slightly raised, revealing a part of her milk white underclothes. Twisting her dissolute body, she appeared to be laughing loudly, her teeth completely exposed, while two short thin men held up her skirt laughing too. At the upper left corner of the picture was an orange-coloured lamp.

I slowly closed my eyes, feeling somewhat afraid to see the woman who painted so explicitly in the colour of golden yellow. Her innermost being must seethe with untold sufferings and intense emotion for her to produce such flaming paintings. It was true that she knew little about painting techniques, but she had a strong sense of colour. It was almost unbelievable that a woman like Auntie Lin who was outwardly so serious in speech and manner could handle the golden yellow—that most brilliant but dangerous of colours—so skilfully. We gazed at each other in silence for a long time. Finally, she bent down to gather the paintings from the floor.

"Why is it that the dancing girl is Chinese and the people on the background are foreign?" I asked suddenly.

"It's a story about a Chinese dancing girl abroad," she said flatly.

"The girl is very charming. Do you know her?"

"She is my daughter Sangsang," she said calmly. "She was hyperactive when she was a small child. When she grew up, she liked to dance, but then she took to smoking cigarettes, drinking alcohol, and finding men. She didn't look like a girl that I could have borne. Both her father and I felt very upset by her behaviour."

"How did she get to go abroad?" I asked again.

"She didn't like school. Even before she entered senior middle school, she followed a few small traders to do business in Guangzhou. Later, she was taken into custody by a public security officer on charges of prostitution. After she was released a year later she met an American businessman who took her to the United States. They got along quite well at the beginning, but later he left her and became a dancing girl in a bar."

"Have you been to the United States to see her?"

"No, never," she said. "I don't want to see her. When her father died he didn't close his eyes. I knew he was still missing the daughter who disappointed him."

"But from your paintings I feel you still cherish profound love for her."

"That's because she'll die soon." Auntie Lin was very miserable. "She wrote me a long letter and posted me several dozen photos of her as a dancing girl. She always wore that long golden skirt. My daughter..." She started sobbing. "She loves this yellow colour so much...."

"What's wrong with her?"

"She had AIDS," Auntie Lin answered. "She even said in her letter that God had granted her the happiest way of dying. She said AIDS was the most beautiful disease to befall the human race."

"She really is no ordinary woman," I said. "But unfortunately, I'll never have the chance to become acquainted with her."

"Even if she is an animal, a dog, a pig, or a fox," Auntie Lin said, "I can't forget her. When I take up my painting brush and begin to paint her, I wish I could forget her. But I don't know why, the more I paint about her the more I miss her."

Just as I was thinking hard as how to say something to comfort

Auntie Lin, Luwei woke up, and his cries drew us from sad mood back to reality. Auntie Lin and I rushed over to him almost at the same time. At the sight of me, Luwei tearfully threw himself into my arms to scratch my face with his tender little hand. All of a sudden, the scene that the little girl, Luwei's sister, held up my leg and did not let me take her baby brother away appeared before my eyes, and a poignant feeling arose from my heart, and I hugged Luwei more tightly.

"I can't forget my daughter because she is my flesh and blood," said Auntie Lin as she was making milk for Luwei. "Although she didn't want to believe she was my daughter, I gave birth to her. Nothing can replace the ties of blood even if it is evil."

Her remarks inadvertently stabbed my heart.

Yu Wei was busy with his business in the company day in, day out. But whenever he had any holidays he would stay together with Luwei from morning till evening. The affection he showed to Luwei when he carried him in his arms often aroused a sad feeling in my heart. Men so irresistibly need progeny! Very often Yu Wei put the child on the carpet and crawled to and fro together with him. The baby laughed excitedly, saliva dripping from the corners of his mouth. We no longer had the time to go for drives in the countryside on Sundays.

Soon Luwei began to grow two snowy white teeth and was able to eat egg yolk. In the process of learning to crawl, he tried to get near the wall, against which he leaned and struggled to stand up to walk one or two steps. But just as he was about to make a step forward, he fell plump back to the floor. By now winter had begun to set in, there was a drop in the temperature. Auntie Lin made Luwei a cotton-padded jacket, a pair of cotton-padded trousers, an undergarment and a pair of beautifully-shaped tiger head shoes. On Sundays she would go back home to clean her uninhabited house and fetch some articles for her own daily use. When she had time she read one or two books I recommended to her. As time went by, the three members of my family all became very fond of her.

However, misfortunes came subtly.

Just before Christmas there came a few successive heavy snowfalls, which turned the streets into a white world. I sat in front of the window to paint the city after snow. With the baby in her arms, Auntie Lin came up to me and asked what the boy was scared of most after he was born. I asked why she asked such a question. She told me: "I carelessly knocked a cassette tape to the ground. The sound was not so loud, but the child's face turned pale with fright."

"Yes, he doesn't deal well with the slightest shock," I said very feebly. "He's a very shy child."

"Perhaps you ate too much fruit when you conceived him," Auntie Lin remarked. "If you ate a bit more meat, I think he might be stronger." She laughed. "I never understood this myself. I heard it from others. But if you ate too much meat, you'd have had a difficult delivery."

"I had a lot of fruit and a lot of meat as well," I said casually.

"Both you and your husband are not young. You're late in having a child. Perhaps it was all for the sake of your career?"

I really did not know why Auntie Lin had become so talkative and so interested in getting to the bottom of things that day. Unable to hide my resentment, I snapped, "Auntie Lin, you'd better not disturb me when I am painting."

She started, her face ashen, and while making an apology to

me, quickly picked up Luwei and withdrew from my studio. The oil paintings she made about her daughter appeared in my mind's eye again. These works, permeated with the unbreakable bonds of motherly love, made me feel sorry for what I had said to her, so I took the initiative in breaking the ice:

"I recommend *The Red Mill* to you to read."

"What's it about?" she asked.

"It's a book about Toulouse-Lautrec, a famous French painter. He had deformed legs and was a dwarf. When he was alive he often went to the Red Mill, a bar, where there were prostitutes and dancing girls. He painted dancing girls superbly well." Then I added: "He was an expert in using the colour red."

"That's the colour for a brothel," she laughed.

Thus ended our temporary estrangement. But it wasn't long before the second unhappy incident came upon us like a flu.

On Christmas Day Yu Wei went to work ahead of time and came home with presents for Luwei, Auntie Lin and me. Unlike people in the West who have turkey on Christmas, we ate roast chicken instead. Seeing us eating meat, Luwei reached out his hand for some. I stopped him for fear that he might get dyspepsia, but Auntie Lin tore off a tiny piece for him, which Luwei swallowed as soon as he got it. As it was Christmas, I did not want to spoil the festival atmosphere, and did not say a word, but at bedtime Auntie Lin suddenly came to me and asked me for photographs of Luwei taken when he was born. "I want to compare what he looked like when he was one month old and a hundred days old."

As if I'd been electrified, I stood there woodenly. Yu Wei quickly walked up and explained: "The child never had any photos taken. We were too busy to take photos of him."

"You certainly didn't make much of a fuss of the child," she said half reproachingly and half regretfully. "I really wanted to see what he looked like a few months ago."

"The New Year will arrive soon, and I promise I'll take a lot of photos of him then," Yu Wei told her laughingly.

As soon as Yu Wei and I went dejectedly to our bedroom, I hastily said that we must fire Auntie Lin, for she had poked her nose into affairs beyond the job of a nurse, interfered with my painting both consciously and unconsciously, and presumptuously decided to give the baby chicken meat to eat. But Yu Wei thought I was being too narrow-minded. According to him, a child mustn't be too finicky, and Auntie Lin wasn't wrong to ask for a look at photographs of Luwei, because she did not know he had not been borne by us.

"Or we just tell her the truth?" Yu Wei suggested.

"No, never."

"It's not your fault that you can't have children," Yu Wei said in a low voice. "Neither is it a defect. You'll feel better if she knows the truth."

"Luwei's destroyed our life," I sobbed. "We seldom have time to be together alone."

"I..." Yu Wei suddenly patted his forehead with the palm of his hand. "Damn me! Well ... next Sunday we'll go for a drive in the countryside."

"What about Luwei?"

"Auntie Lin'll look after him."

"But we can't go to Bafangtai this time."

"Of course." Yu Wei switched off the bedside reading lamp and murmured in my ear: "Santa Claus told me a man must dedicate the best of his body to the woman he loves most tonight."

"Santa Claus's told me a woman mustn't accept any present from a man rashly." I lay in his warm embrace receiving his tender love. The window lattices rustled, and the cold wind, for the sake of our fire-like passion, had suddenly changed its nature: it's like the soft feeler of spring wind.

4. The Mysterious Old Shepherd

It had been over two years since Yu Wei and I began going for a drive in the countryside on Sundays. His company had a reliable jeep. If the weather was fine I would usually take my painting paraphernalia as well as bread, sausages and beer. Both Yu Wei and I loved nature and would stay in the open country till the sun had set in the west and evening had crept in deep around us.

We woke up early this Sunday and heard Auntie Lin awake and chatting to Luwei. They always woke up earlier than us.

"You naughty little child," Auntie Lin teased Luwei by way of complaining. "Who wet the bed last night?"

The little baby answered back with a "yi ya" and from time to time produced a "pu, pu" sound in his mouth, because he was growing teeth and his gums were itchy. Auntie Lin said, "Oh, that's not right. There's a good boy. Give your granny a scratch..." Luwei had learned to scratch with his hand in a symbolic way. Perhaps he made a prompt response, for we heard Auntie Lin exclaim in great excitement: "A good scratch, a good scratch." It was followed by the boy's chuckling and crying.

After we got up, we played with Luwei for a while and then asked Auntie Lin to look after him well before we set out for the countryside beyond the suburbs. Once our jeep was out of the city, there was little traffic on the road. The people we occasionally passed on the road all shrank back from the cold wind.

Yu Wei slowed the jeep down as he turned to ask me, "Where shall we go?"

One village that was fairly close to the city was Fish Pagoda which was beyond Bafangtai Village. Bafangtai and Fish Pagoda lay about twenty kilometres apart but were two poor riverside villages. Both villages had been quite well-known in the vicinity. It was said that there was not one man in Fish Pagoda who didn't like gambling. Evidence of this was that not a decent house could be seen in the village; all the houses with adobe walls were slanting or collapsed, their broken windows covered with plastic sheets. There were no fences in front of the courtyards. Not a soul could be seen. It seemed the whole village had died out. We drove through slowly. Finally, we found an ox standing beside a public convenience, covered by white frosting of cold, and then at the western end of the village, a flock of sheep were vying with each other to eat something in a tumult in the pen beside one house.

"There's a spark of life at long last!" Yu Wei stopped the jeep.

I watched the scrabbling sheep with the utmost concentration. They had once been white but due to dirt and murky weather, their original colour had become rather indeterminable.

"Why doesn't every household here raise sheep?" I asked. "There are plenty of pastures nearby. And mutton's expensive too."

"Perhaps the people here don't even have the funds to raise sheep," Yu Wei remarked.

"It seems this household is the richest in the village," I said jokingly. "Look, the house's red brick, and the doorframe is painted blue."

"I guess the host of this house must have a good moral character," Yu Wei said. "I'm sure he's not a gambler. Otherwise he'd have lost the sheep long ago."

"Perhaps it's just the opposite," I told Yu Wei. "I think the host of the house must be a big gambler who never loses. And because his gambling skill is so good he's won all the sheep of the village."

"Oh!" Yu Wei was taken aback. "That's one possibility."

Just as we were guessing wildly, the eye-catching blue gate was pushed open, and an old man of about seventy years old emerged. Short and thin, he was dressed in tatters, a sparse white beard on his chin, and a dark felt hat on his head. He had a brandy nose and beady eyes, which were blank when he looked at people. Yu Wei quickly lowered the glass of the window, intending to strike up a conversation with him.

The old man walked up to the pen and cursed the sheep: "You've started an internal strife all for the sake of a bean cake. You call yourselves brothers?"

These remarks set us laughing in our sleeve. After having cursed the sheep, the old man walked toward us slowly. Yu Wei greeted him warmly: "Grandpa, your family must be very rich; you own so large a flock of sheep."

The old man cast a glance at Yu Wei before he walked silently around our jeep toward its rear. What was he doing walking to the rear? "He must have some mental problem," I said jokingly.

"I don't think so," Yu Wei said. "He's just eccentric. Sometimes you're like that."

I poked my head out of the window and saw the old man lying

on the ground to look at the rear number plate. "I was right. He's a head case. He's lying on the ground to see the number plate."

Yu Wei opened the door and got out. "What are you looking at the number plate for, grandpa?" he asked.

"Oh, yes..." the old man said as he scrambled up from the ground and brushed off the dust on his hands. "I learned a few Arabic numerals when I was young. I wanted to see if I still remembered them."

"Can you still remember them?" Yu Wei asked, smiling.

"I've a bad memory." The old man still rubbed his hands. "I can't remember them all."

I also got out the jeep and smiled at him.

"Are you from the city?" the old man asked.

"Yes, we came here just for a drive," Yu Wei and I answered in unison.

"Why don't you come in and sit awhile?" The old man suddenly became warm toward us. "Come in and have a bowl of water. My grandson, granddaughter-in-law and great grandson all are home. My granddaughter-in-law has just baked some melon seeds."

Following him, we entered his house. It was spacious, bright and clean inside. Everything was in neat order. As we walked in, a boy of about three years old was leaning against the door-jamb smiling at us. The old man's grandson was weaving bird-cages using thin iron wire. The old man's granddaughter-in-law was a plump woman, who had her hair trimmed short to the ear. She had a flat nose, a broad forehead and thick lips. At the left corner of her mouth there was a mole. She had a lucky face although she was not particularly beautiful. She dished up a plate of melon seeds she had just baked to us.

"You're a very fortunate man, grandpa," Yu Wei said to the old man. "You even have a great grandson now."

The old man spat before he said, "We weren't like you at that time. We got married in our teens and had children when we were young. I became a father when I was only seventeen."

"You live with your grandson, but where is your son?" I asked.

"My son?" The old man shone a sad look in his eyes. Then he said with a sigh, "He'd died a long time ago. He liked to gamble but couldn't afford to lose. He drowned himself in the river ten years ago."

"I'm sorry," I said hastily. "I shouldn't have asked that question to make you feel sad."

"No, I don't feel sad." The old man shook his hand. "Ten families gambled, ten families would be ruined. It's all right that he died. But my grandson is a good man, who has always engaged in honest work. He's even a primary school graduate." He harped on happily: "You go and have a look around Fish Pagoda. We're the only ones who keep livestock. We have a flock of sheep and a head of cattle."

I was reminded of the ox standing by the public convenience. That must be the cattle the old man mentioned.

"We fare better at farming than others in summer," the old man continued.

"My grandpa even goes hunting in autumn," the young woman put in with a smile.

"Life is like that," the old man concluded. "If you work hard, you'll have a better life; if you ruin your life, your days will become harder for you."

"My grandpa always talks about big principles," the young man who was as thin as his grandpa said as he handed two bowls of water to us. Then, pointing to the melon seeds in the plate, he continued to say, "They were grown in our garden. Help yourself." With that he walked out of the house.

I snatched up a handful of melon seeds and, while cracking them, made for the window, from where I saw the old man's grandson first walk to the sheep pen to throw a bundle of hay and then go to our jeep and circle it before he stopped in front to read the figures on the front number plate. He has some schooling and is sure to recognise all those numerals, I thought to myself.

The old man began to tell us the history of Fish Pagoda: people here lived on fishing and farming, and their families were rather well-off. It was purely because they were rich that the villagers became bored when they had nothing to do in the slackness of winter, so they got together to play cards to pass the time. At the beginning they played cards just for amusement and later they started to gamble. As a result, Fish Pagoda became poorer and poorer with each passing day; people loved ease but hated work, all the men became inveterate smokers, and everyone became gluttonous and lazy. When the highly skilled gamblers in other villages learned that villagers in Fish Pagoda were fond of gambling, they came here and won over everything that was worth a penny.

The old man filled the bowl of his smoking pipe with tobacco before he continued with narrowed eyes: "You don't know what a tragic scene it was when the villagers' property was being taken away. Children cried and housewives moaned. In the past almost every household raised dogs, but did you hear any dog barking when you entered the village?" The old man stopped for a while and then made the answer himself: "No, no dog barks anymore. Of course, it's no use having dogs. The purpose of keeping dogs is to look after the house. Now that only breathing people are left in the house all day, what do you need the dog for?" The old man was in deep sorrow. "Last spring the government sent a work team here to help the poor. They went from household to household asking the villagers to quit gambling. They pointed out that the village is close to the city, and if they grew vegetables to sell in the city, they would not be poor anymore. Most of the villagers listened. Unfortunately, Heaven did not help. In summer there was a hailstone storm that ruined the crops, and in autumn the vegetables were drowned by floods."

"On our way here we saw that every door was shut tight. Are the villagers still sleeping?" I asked.

"They gambled a whole night last night, so both adults and children are tired." The old man spat. "In winter time the day is short. Get up late and they can save firewood and rice. If you don't believe what I say, you can go out and have a look around. Except for my house, who else's chimney is smoking at the moment in this village?" Then he added decisively: "None!"

"You're even worse off here than in Bafangtai Village," I responded.

"Bafangtai?" the old man asked indifferently. "Have you been there?"

"We only heard about it," Yu Wei prevaricated quickly.

"That village is much richer than this one here," the old man confessed.

Then the old man made detailed inquiries of us about our work, life and children, and we answered his questions one by one. "I've met painters," he told us. "When summer arrives they come to the pastureland with an easel on their back and sit painting a whole day there. If you want to paint about Fish Pagoda, you'd better choose to paint the flock of sheep of ours. I have an adopted son." He came to a sudden halt, and his granddaughter-in-law hastily found an excuse and left by dragging the child along with her. The old man continued: "My adopted son lives in somewhere else. He's a kind-hearted and highly skilled man. He started herding sheep while he was still a child. Although it's snowing hard outside, if he were here, he could drive the entire pen of sheep to the vast wild pasture. If you painted that scene, it'd be a beautiful picture."

I had never imagined that this old man who talked wild and was dressed in rags could say something so profound about art. "When will he come?" I asked hastily.

"He—" The old man rolled his eyes rapidly. "By this time next Sunday, I guess."

"I'll come to wait for him here next Sunday," I told the old man.

"You don't need to come here. You can drive your jeep to the vast wild pasture directly. Your vehicle is good and can run in the wild. By then you will see him driving a flock of sheep in the open countryside. He can also sing songs. His singing is very moving indeed."

What a legendary figure it was! He could drive a whole pen of sheep to float on the vast cold pastureland in winter and sing songs in the dry chilly wind. This temptation was irresistible for us.

After bidding goodbye to the old man, we drove to the wilderness, where pathways lay zigzagged on the ground. Heavy snow had turned it white. Dry withered grass and mugworts beside the road shook in the cold wind, the nearby river had frozen over, all was quiet and solitary, not a sheet of cloud and not a trace of man or bird could be seen. The wilderness was so boundless and lonesome. Drowning in it, Yu Wei and I swept our glances across the land before we got out of the jeep and started a walk in the wind. The houses in the distant Fish Pagoda Village appeared like a large stretch of scattered balls of horse dung, very few wisps of cooking smoke were seen rising from the chimneys atop the houses.

After we returned to the jeep and ate some food we turned our thought to Auntie Lin and Luwei. It had been only half a day since we left home, but we began to miss the child. So about three o'clock in the afternoon, we started to drive back to the city. When we passed through Fish Pagoda I saw a man taking his wife and child to the house of another family. Wearing cumbersome clothes, they shrank their heads, hid their hands in the sleeves and shrugged their shoulders just like bears coming out from winter sleep in the caves of trees.

5. The Appearance of the Shepherd

The atmospheric pressure was rather low on the day we went back to Fish Pagoda Village. There was no sunshine, no wind. The weather forecast said it would snow in the afternoon, but snow came before noon. The road ahead was extremely murky, so we had to drive very slowly.

"Damn!" I cursed. "I've brought my paints in vain. How could the old man's adopted son come back in weather like this?"

"Then you paint the landscape in the snow." Yu Wei always

found something to comfort me when I was in low spirits. "It'll be much more sentimental than sitting by the window to paint the buildings in the city." He encouraged me with a smile: "Maybe the old man's adopted son has already driven sheep to the open country. Don't lose heart."

Feeling warmed inside, I cocked my head towards him. "You're so good to me, Yu Wei. Do you want me to be dead set on following you in my next life?"

"Don't talk inauspiciously," Yu Wei responded. "If a next life really exists, I wouldn't choose a person like you to be my wife. It's too much like hard work!" He laughed wilfully. "You're too arrogant and formidable."

Laughing and bantering, we drove into Fish Pagoda. By now snowfall had gained momentum. When we passed by the old man's home, I noticed there was no sheep in the pen. My morale boosted, I urged Yu Wei to drive faster.

As we moved out of the village, we did not see any flock of sheep at first. What took form in the whiteness was a dark shadow dancing in the blizzard. It was only when the jeep drew near that we could discern a man standing in the snow with a whip in his hand and gazing at us. Surrounding him was a large flock of sheep, which were moving slowly forward over the snow-covered ground.

Both Yu Wei and I were stupefied. We stopped our jeep and gazed at the scene before us with bated breath. Through the hazy glass of the window, I saw the man was flicking his whip and the sheep were moving around him. The sky, the earth, the air and the flock of sheep were all white, only the man provided a dark contrast, which was a startling focal point. This was the first time I really understood the significance of dark colours. I forgot about painting; I had been transported into another world. As if obsessed, I stared at the dazzling dark colour sharply contrasted against that powerful white backdrop until the snow let up slightly and the shepherd was driving the flock of sheep toward our vehicle.

I opened the door and walked towards him. There was no wind for it had abruptly died down completely. The sun remained hidden. It was rather quiet in the snow-covered country. I heard the resounding crunching the sheep produced as they walked on the snow. A thin middle-aged man stood in front of us with a gloomy look on his face.

"Were you painting me and the flock of sheep in the jeep all the time?" He fixed his big, deep-set eyes at me. I could hardly believe a man could have such keen eyes.

"I painted nothing. I only watched," I told him. "Did you know we'd come today?"

"My uncle told me you'd come," he answered. "I've been here a long time."

"We wondered on our way here if you'd come on a snowy day like this?" I pointed to the sheep that appeared to be shivering with cold. "How can they stand the cold?"

"Sheep are better insulated than people." The man's mouth twitched. "They wear a layer of fur."

"Heard you like to graze the sheep here on Sundays?"

"Yes, I only come here on Sundays. I love sheep."

"Where do you live?" I asked. "Is your home far from here?"

"Not far." He hesitated. "I work as a carpenter for a building company. They hired me."

"I heard you can sing well?"

The expression in his eyes dimmed, and he lowered his head.

"But you can't paint my voice on canvas."

"Yes, I can."

"Really?" He shook his head bashfully. "It's impossible."

"You sing me a song and see," I said.

His Adam's apple twitched and his lips moved as though he was about to sing. But when he opened his mouth again, it was not a song but a question about what time we had set off from the city and whether we had children at home.

I told him we had set off immediately after breakfast and we had a lovely son at home who was nine months old.

"Is he a noisy boy?" He seemed to have a keen interest in children.

"He used to be," I told him laughingly. "But now he is a good boy. He eats well and sleeps soundly and smiles a lot."

"Can he walk now?" he asked again.

At that moment Yu Wei came over to us.

"He can't yet. But he can stand up by leaning against the wall."

"Some children start to walk very late. It's not something to worry about," he said in a mild tone as he squatted down to caress a sheep's head with his hands. He seemed curiously awkward at the sight of Yu Wei. I hastily introduced him to my husband. But when Yu Wei reached out his hand to him, he uneasily put his hands into the sleeves of his padded jacket.

"You're rich," he mumbled in a low voice. "You have a jeep to drive."

"This jeep I've borrowed from my company. It doesn't belong to me," Yu Wei explained to him. "I can only drive it at certain times."

"At least you have a vehicle to drive and don't have to work at home on Sundays." He stood up and kicked the snow on the ground. "Who looks after your child when you are out?"

"We have a nurse," I told him.

"Is the nurse old or young?" he asked further.

"An old nurse," I answered.

"It's better to have an old nurse," he said. "Old nurses have patience."

He looked at us with fear, suspicion and sorrow in his eyes as though we were two hanged ghosts. We were struck with ill ease. After a long while, he unbuttoned the top part of his padded jacket and removed a string of wooden beads from his neck. He weighed the beads in the palm of his hand before he gave it to me and said, "Please, take this back to your child to play with."

It was a string of beads exquisitely made out of white birch wood. The beads were extremely round and smooth. I took them, and thanked him profusely but he said hastily, "You don't need to thank me. I love children. When you come again I'll make a wooden car and bear for your child." Casting a swift glance at me, he continued: "You must keep the beads as their original colour. Don't colour them with any paint or dyestuff. Those things are harmful. Children don't understand this. Your son will put the beads in his mouth."

We nodded our heads.

The sheep began to run along the perimetre of the open country. The shepherd shouted at the top of his lungs: "Stop— stop—" His voice was hoarse but powerful, but the sheep kept moving forward.

"These sheep will return to Fish Pagoda by themselves," the shepherd told us.

"Your uncle is indeed a formidable man," Yu Wei remarked. "Fish Pagoda is a famous poor village, and most of the villagers love to gamble, but no one dares to steal the sheep your uncle keeps in the pen."

"There are people who tried that." The shepherd smiled. "But they're afraid of my formidable uncle so no one dares to go near the sheep." When he talked about the flock of sheep and his uncle, his face brightened up, and he looked at Yu Wei and I with much milder eyes.

"Are you married?" Yu Wei asked.

The shepherd shrugged his shoulder and twitched his nose. "Of course."

"Do you have children?" Yu Wei asked again.

"Of course." The man twitched his nose and shrugged his shoulder again. His expression seemed to jeer at us for our stupidity. Isn't it right and proper for a mature man to get married and have children? Is it necessary to ask such questions?

When we wanted to make an appointment to meet him again, he said, "I'm not certain when I can come, but I'm certain that when I come, it will be on a Sunday. It's very beautiful here when spring comes. Wild flowers are everywhere. You should bring your child here."

"That's a good idea," Yu Wei exclaimed. "We'll bring our child here when spring comes."

The shepherd subtly smiled before he raised his hand to wave goodbye. He walked away very slowly and wearily in the direction of Fish Pagoda.

"We have met a very mysterious man!" I said.

"So don't think that only the realm of art has mysterious people," Yu Wei joked.

It looked as if to justify Yu Wei's judgment, the quiet snow-bound wilderness suddenly gave a quiver, and together with it came the loud and clear singing of songs.

6. Sangsang's Story

"Sangsang had a clear voice when she was a child, and loved to imitate the singing of birds, twittering all day long. She did not stop even during meals. Careless in handling things, she frequently dropped basins, broke bowls, or did her buttons up in wrong positions. She liked to play pranks. Once she hid her grandfather's small-bowled long-stemmed tobacco pipe in a flower vase. We searched for it high and low, all in vain. Nobody would have thought the pipe had been hidden among flowers in the vase.

"Sangsang liked to adorn herself. When she saw other girls wearing new clothes, she asked for new clothes; when she caught sight of someone with painted finger nails, she wanted to follow suit. At the time she was four or five, every morning she asked me to paint a bean-like mark on her forehead with the red ink-paste used for seals, otherwise she refused to eat. She was also greedy for dainties, and that was why she had a poor appetite when she grew up.

"Sangsang's father and I were very busy with our work, and we did not have time to teach her how to behave. She developed an interest in dancing when she was only three or four years old. Even then she was good at pirouettes. Once, wearing a white skirt she pirouetted in front of me swiftly with her arms spreading out, while laughingly counting the turns she made. She did not stop until I was dizzy and only felt a haze of white clouds dancing before me.

"When Sangsang went to primary school she joined the school's dance group, and at home after school she often imitated ballet dancers, running around on tiptoe like those in *Swan Lake*. She continued to adorn herself, and paid little attention to her lessons. She often bickered with her schoolmates and that was why she had very few friends during her childhood. In the third year she had to stay down, but she did not care a fig. Once her mathematics teacher asked her to perform a mathematical calculation on the blackboard. She held a piece of chalk in hand and stood before the blackboard at a loss. The teacher walked up to her and said ironically, "If you can't even do such a simple calculation, what can you do?" Lifting her eyebrows, Sangsang threw the chalk away, and without saying a word, started humming a song and began to dance right on the platform. While dancing, she said provocatively to the teacher, "I can dance! I can dance!" The whole class was thrown into a tumult; boys started whistling and girls giggled. The teacher stood by awkwardly until she finished dancing. When Sangsang returned to her seat, the teacher said with rage to the whole class, "Pupils like Sangsang should be expelled from the school." Sangsang was so angry she threw her pencil box to the ground in protest. Consequently, both Sangsang's father and I were summoned by the principal to the school to discuss the matter. Only after we pleaded time and again, did the school agree not to expel her. But because Sangsang liked to play pranks and make trouble in the class, no class wanted to have her, and she gained a bad reputation throughout the school.

"When she was in the fourth year, for a period of time Sangsang often came home from school in low spirits. She neither talked to her father nor spoke with me. When we ate dinner she would take her share of food to her room and eat alone there. We did not know what had happened to her. One weekend, as she was about to take food to her room again, I could not hold myself anymore and said scoldingly, "Sangsang, why don't you eat together with us? Are your father and mother so repellant to you?"

"Without saying a word, Sangsang went to her room with a bowl of rice in her hands. After she had finished eating, she came out with arms akimbo and suddenly pointed an accusing finger at me: "You are not my real mother. You have no right to tell me what to do anymore!"

"I almost fainted hearing that. If I wasn't her mother, who was? When I asked her how she had come by such a fanciful idea, she laughed and pointed at me: "Are you afraid to admit it? Just find a mirror and look at yourself. Is there any resemblance between you and me? You're small-eyed, I'm big-eyed; your eyebrows are sparse, while mine are dark and thick; your mouth is so small that it looks like a chicken's ass, while mine is big; you always speak weakly, but I'm full of strength. How could a woman like you give birth to me, Sangsang? No one knows where you got me? Probably you murdered my real parents and changed my name and made me your daughter. Many people say Sangsang doesn't look like Lin Huixian's daughter. If other people can say that to me, why do you still try to fool me?" Then Sangsang burst into tears and wept grievously. I did not know how she had become suspicious of her origin. From then on she refused to talk to me and often asked my colleagues behind my back about where I had got her. My colleagues thought Sangsang had psychological problems and advised me to take her to see a psychiatrist or to dissolve her suspicions with tender motherly feeling. I did my utmost to show her warmth and concern, but the result was just the opposite to what I had wished. Whenever I gave her some loving attention, she would lift her eyebrows and say sarcastically, "Are you feeling guilty? You refuse to tell me about my own father and mother, but sooner or later, I'll find them!"

"Sangsang went to the hospital to have her blood tested and then came home to compare her blood type with mine. When she found out my blood was also "O" type, she said to me, "Just look at your ugly face. How can you have the same 'O' type blood as I? You're cheating!" Then she began to inquire about in which hospital she was born and which midwife attended the birth. When she found out the midwife had died in a traffic accident, she thought there was a great conspiracy behind the whole story, and began to suspect everything. After she started junior middle school, she often cut classes, so every three or four days her class teacher called me to the school to give me a dressing down, complaining that I had not disciplined my daughter well. I had to search for her everywhere. During one such search I found her dancing beside a dustbin. It was summer time. Sandals in hand, she danced barefooted, surrounded by a group of nasty boys who were clapping their hands for her. An old garbage collector was collecting money from the audience in a wornout straw hat. The scene angered me, and I walked up to Sangsang and slapped her in the face as she danced. She squatted down, covered her face with her hands, without saying a word for quite some time. The old man indignantly reproached me: "How did you dare to beat Sangsang? She's a kind-hearted girl with no one to rely on. She often comes here to dance so as to help me earn some small change." I told the old man: "I beat

Sangsang because she is my daughter." The old man looked at me in surprise: "What? You're Sangsang's mother? But she told me she's an orphan!" I was so angry, I fell in a dead faint on the street. Some passers-by sent me to hospital, but Sangsang put on her sandals and disappeared with some of the boys.

"After that, Sangsang often spent the whole night outside. She painted her lips bright red. When she came back home to fetch something, she would look at me with sidelong glances. Once she went home and happened to find her father painting bamboo. With a glance at the painting, she said sneeringly, "Why paint the poor bamboo? Bamboo is empty inside. A sham! Why should people praise it for its being straight and lofty?" With that she unleashed a torrent of abuse against the model essays in her text books which, according to her, were nothing but nonsense. She particularly loathed those short articles which were written to express ideals through describing some objects and which had been acclaimed for generations. She called them simply dog shit. Her father was so enraged, he threw half a bottle of ink in her face and asked her to get out and never come back home again. Indeed, she did not come home for a whole summer nor the following autumn. Her teachers said that if they had the opportunity to see Sangsang in the school they felt more honoured than all those imperial beauties of the back palaces meeting the emperor in ages past. Then Sangsang fell in love and moved in with her boyfriend. Of course, I learned this later, because I knew doctors at the hospital where Sangsang went to have her abortion. That year she was sixteen. A sixteen-year-old girl having abortion! You can just imagine how agonised I felt at heart!

"Early in winter that year, when it began to get cold, I unpicked and washed her padded jacket and trousers and lined them with some new cotton. Then I went out to look for her everywhere, and left a message with the families to whom I thought she would possibly go: Sangsang, please go back to Lin Huixian's home soon. I emphasised Lin Huixian's home rather than her parents' home, for I was afraid she wouldn't go back at all because of her defiant nature. My message worked. One dark evening, when the northwest wind was blowing hard, just after we had finished eating our supper, Sangsang came back. She was terribly thin, and still wearing autumn clothes. Her lips were frozen purple. I made a big bowl of hot noodle soup for her. She wolfed down the bowl of noodles quickly and then played with the spoon by licking it. In a quiet voice, she asked: "Lin Huixian, what did you ask me to come back for?" Suppressing my anger, I told her that it was getting cold and she must have her padded clothes. She raised her eyebrows and blew at her nail: "Is that all?" I told her that I had something else to say to her. She laughed ironically before saying, "I knew you'd confess your sins in time. Finally you're going to admit you are not my own parents." I told her: "Quite the contrary. We are your real parents. Otherwise we wouldn't care for you so much." In referring to the abortion she had had behind our back, I said, "You are only sixteen. But why did you let it happen so early..." I wanted to persuade her to change her ways. But to my surprise, she pounded the table in indignation and shouted: "It's me who had the abortion, not you. Why were you so worried about it? I'll do what I like. It has nothing to do with you." Her father lost control again and slapped her face. Sangsang cast a queer glance at her father before she went to her room without saying a word in retort. We locked her door from the outside. "We'll keep you in custody at home rather than let you go out to do damage to others in the society." Her father gripped the key in his hand, resolving not to let Sangsang move even half a step out of the house. He would keep a close watch on her even if it meant he did not go to work. We heard Sangsang jumping, cursing, kicking the door in her room until midnight when she quieted down. We thought she had tired herself out and fallen asleep. Her father lay awake all night that night. The next morning, after we prepared breakfast, we unlocked the door and called her out to eat, but we found no trace of her. It was very cold in the room, a sealed window had been opened, a rope that had been made by jointing torn pieces of a bed sheet together was flying outside the window from a central heating pipe. She had torn a brand-new bed sheet into small pieces. We lived in the third floor; she had climbed down from the cord. Sangsang's limbs were very nimble, and when she danced, her movements were lithe and graceful. I thought that once she left this time, she would never come back. The padded jacket and trousers I had devoted time and energy to making for her had been put in the corner of the room; the padded trousers stood erect against the wall like two chopped-off legs. On the padded clothes Sangsang left a note, which read: Comrades Xin Changfeng and Lin Huixian, do you think you keep me at home like a hostage? My world is very wide. The padded jacket and trousers Lin Huixian made for me are ridiculously loose. The trousers even can stand on the floor. Can you call it cotton-lined padded jacket? No, these clothes seem to be made of iron. If in the future Lin Huixian should make padded clothes for her own daughter, she shouldn't line them so thickly. Winter is not that frightful.

"Since then Sangsang never came home again, nor did she go to school. Later, I heard she went with someone to Guangzhou and spent her time laughing and joking together with men, not bothering about personal dignity. Then, she was arrested for prostitution. It was not that she was short of money. It was as she said when she was interrogated that she wanted to see the ugly features of men in paying her money and making love to her. For that purpose she made a reckless move. During the Spring Festival that year she was put in prison, her father and I were so broken-hearted that we could not eat the traditional family-reunion dumplings. We wanted to go to see her—in spite of everything she had been really a lovely girl when she was small—yet she had broken our hearts.

"While living abroad, she would not have written to me if she were not going to die. In the letter she addressed me by name instead of calling me mother. Even so, her writing to me was a compromise itself. She had begun to suspect her origins from her childhood, had no confidence in the world around her, and took a strong rebellious attitude toward it. She did not like all the things that ran in the regular order of society and preferred to be at liberty to enjoy herself, with a keen interest in all social misfits and outcasts. I often thought to myself that if we had taught her properly before she reached five or six and had not winked at her and let her feel it was perfectly justified for her to have everything her own way, she might not have developed into what she is today. She might even have become a well-trained ballet dancer who gave performances in a big theatre, and the happy wife of a loving husband. But she had destroyed all this very easily. It seemed she liked the air in bars better, preferring to dance for a few men who were interested in her. In her letter she said she was very happy when she heard men call her "a bitch whore". On the back of the photographs she posted to me were cosmetics stains, which indicated that she still loved to wear heavy makeup. To her, death would come as a relief; living was suffering.

"I still did not know why Sangsang had so flatly refused to be our daughter. After so many years had drearily passed, I suddenly felt that she was not my daughter, the blood that ran through her body was not mine. But who had brought her into the world? Why was she so strongly against me? Sometimes I thought: if I were Sangsang and suspected my parents were not my own father and mother, would I be so hostile to them? I thought I would not. But Sangsang would, because she was Sangsang.

"...But why did my poor daughter Sangsang behave that way? She was born in early spring... She was just ... over thirty... She liked ... the colour of golden yellow... She loved to dance..."

7. The Shadow

Luwei had brought me back to the earthly, noisy, worrisome but lovely world. I began to put my heart and soul into his affairs. He had grown a few teeth and could do whatever was suggested to him. Once he had a cold and ran a high fever. In the dead of night Yu Wei and I took him to hospital. It was only on the third day after his fever was gone that I found myself in the mood to eat. To watch a child grow was really marvellous; I could discern Luwei's every change at any moment. He was fond of water, hot-tempered, and when he woke up and felt hungry, would burst out crying nonstop if Auntie Lin was slow in preparing milk for him.

That I first hit Luwei took place at the last weekend of February. It was because of an accident with his milk. After he had woken up, Auntie Lin quickly warmed up some milk, poured it into a feeding bottle and handed it to him. He was so enraged by then, he reached out his little hand to scratch Auntie Lin's face and knocked the feeding bottle to the ground. I snatched him from Auntie Lin's arms, put him on his little cot and slapped him on the backside. At each slap I gave the child, Auntie Lin cried piercingly: "Stop! He already knew he was wrong." Luwei cried so mournfully, he almost fainted. After that, he became very obedient when he was given the feeding bottle. After all, I didn't want Sangsang's tragedy to occur in my family but it was just because of this matter that Yu Wei had a fierce quarrel with me. That day after he came back from work, I felt complacent and told him how I had brought Luwei under control: "A small child like him even knew how to scratch people, just because he was hungry and the milk was a bit late. How could I bear to see him behaving like that? A few slaps from me and he knew what was right." I pointed to Luwei as I talked. That evening Luwei was obviously in low spirits and very indignant when he saw me. Yu Wei's face turned pale with rage when he heard what I said. This was the first time he made me feel embarrassed in front of others. "Do you think that a woman of thirty subduing a child less than one year old is something to be proud of?" He pointed at my nose and said in a trembling voice, "He is a small child, yet you try to restrain him from developing his own individual character. What person do you want him to be? A moral hypocrite? A womanish eunuch? You can't use an adult's views to restrict a baby. That's unfair!"

"If he refused to accept the feeding milk bottle now, he would refuse all he should accept later," I retorted out of self-respect although I felt humiliated. "Bad habits are the accumulation of daily disobedience you know."

"Do you expect he could take up a paint brush proficiently immediately after he was born?"

"Please don't mock my profession." I started to cry. "Perhaps the countryside is a better place for him to grow up. Over there, he has his sister and brother, a small courtyard and crickets. He'll understand things are not come by easily, and he'll treasure them." I sobbed hysterically: "What shall we give to him over here? Affection without the ties of blood? Desolate city and narrow streets? Or the lifeless living apartment which looks like a cinerary casket? Yes, in terms of material needs, he will have all things that country children have not, but he has lost fresh air and simple and honest kinship. Do you know why he brushed off the feeding bottle?" I blurted out: "He wanted to suck the breasts of his own mother!"

Auntie Lin, her face ashen, carried the still crying Luwei out of the room. My head buzzed. Good Heavens! What had I said? I was telling her Luwei was not my own child! But he was my child. Every grin and smile of his brought me excitement and joy. Perhaps Sangsang's story was too heavy a load on my mind.

"I know, it's I who's brought these troubles to you." Yu Wei made an apology to me after a long silence, but his apology was meaningless to me. Auntie Lin already knew Luwei was my adopted son. How would she look at me, a female painter who could not bear children?

That evening I did not go back to my bedroom. I sat woodenly alone in my dark studio gazing out the window. It was dark outside. To defend my self-esteem, when friends had asked why we had no child although we had married for many years, Yu Wei had always said humorously that he loved me so much that he did not want to have a child to interfere in our love, and I had stalled them off with a vague answer that I wanted to live a carefree life while I was still young. In order to adopt a child, Yu Wei had naively made a tentative plan; he asked me to go to stay in a friend's home in the countryside for a period of time and then he would tell others that I was pregnant and went to rest there. Nobody would suspect that I had adopted a baby a few months old after I had stayed away for some time. I made a flat refusal to his plan right away. Consequently Luwei's arrival put me in a very awkward position. A few days ago, two artist friends whom I had not met for more than a year came to see me, and when they suddenly saw Luwei in the cot, asked suspiciously: "You've such a big son?" I just laughed and nodded my head, without making any explanation, and under their surprised eyes, prattled with Luwei affectionately like mother and son. At his company, Yu Wei just told others he already had a son but did not say he had an adopted son. All friends in his company regarded me as a person who could come and go like a shadow and it would not be surprising that such a woman had suddenly had a child. They probably talked about it and did a lot of guesswork behind our backs, but they made a pretence of ignorance in front of us. Yu Wei and I needed such kind of pretence, which was the gentle and soft light penetrating the window paper and which gave me a sense of illusion; if the window paper was torn open, the dazzling light would flood in to wound my heart. I had never thought that it would be me who ripped open the window paper. This kind of paper was too fragile.

It was a deep night. Beams of faint light came up the window now and then, traffic was still on in the streets. The bitter wind chilled me to the bone, and the image of Sangsang began to appear before my eyes. When Auntie Lin tearfully told me Sangsang's story that winter afternoon, I felt deeply pained. Sangsang deliberately went to extremes just because she was suspicious of her own parents, what would Luwei do when he knew the truth after he grew up? Would he leave us, or would he give himself up as hopeless?

The studio door was pushed open lightly, and in came Auntie Lin. In soft steps she walked slowly to me and sat on the stool before me. Her decrepit appearance looked very moving in the darkness.

"Luwei has gone to sleep," she said in a hoarse voice. "He was still sobbing when he fell into sleep. He felt greatly wronged."

Auntie Lin also blamed me. "I shouldn't have told you about Sangsang that day," she said slowly. "If I have known Luwei wasn't your own child, I wouldn't have told you the story. I didn't want to hurt you on purpose."

I made no response. I wanted to hear what else she would say.

"Sangsang's an exception to ordinary people," she continued. "In reality girls like her are few and far between. I often fatalistically thought that it was her own instinctive nature that brought her down. She would not have been able to live like most people do even if she had received good education. Some people are born moral degenerates and drug addicts. You can't say they are forced into it by life's burdens or are seduced by others. They like to behave that way. No one can stop them."

Auntie Lin paused to heave a sigh of relief before she went on:

"Recently I began to think: Sangsang must have regarded us as her own parents from the bottom of her heart, but because her life style was entirely different from ours, she wanted to break totally away from us, so she presumed we were not her own parents. She used this as an excuse for her rebellious behaviour."

"You mean she purposely made up an excuse for herself?" I asked.

"Yes, I think that's the way it was. But as time went by, she became more and more sure that her suspicion was fact and then she was forced to believe it."

"But you said she had been indulged in her childhood. No one had done a thing against her will. Should she have been spoilt like that when she was a small child, she would have grown into an attentive girl."

"Luwei is different," Auntie Lin said. "He's less than one year old."

"But he already knew how to refuse what his instinct told him to have. He was very hungry then and wanted to have milk. But when the milk was a bit late, he raised his hand and knocked the feeding bottle away. Anyway, this was not a good omen," I said, heavy-hearted.

Auntie Lin was speechless. I could not see the expression on her face clearly, I could only discern the outline. But from her uneven breathing, I sensed she was very agitated.

"Don't worry," she said to me. "I won't tell anyone about Luwei. In fact he is your child already. Don't think about it too much." Auntie Lin hesitated for a moment. "Yu Wei is very nice to you. I've never seen a husband like him who gives so much close consideration to his wife. What he said in the evening was a bit too harsh. Don't take it to heart. Anyway he's already apologised."

I made no response. Auntie Lin stood up and left. Sitting in the darkness, I felt my head swimming. It was the first time I had raised a hand to Luwei, and I hit him rightly. As a matter of fact, I had already taken him as my own child. But then did I slap him too heavily? Would he refuse to let me hold him tomorrow?

I left home quietly before daybreak. In winter the sun came out very late. Street lights were still on. There were very few people and sparse traffic on the street as I headed for the distant bus station with the intention of walking alone in the wilderness beyond Fish Pagoda. Perhaps, the flock of sheep there would give me new confidence and warmth.

The only long-distance bus that was going to Chutianba passed by Fish Pagoda Village, but that regular bus service started after eight o'clock, so I went to a restaurant beside the bus station to get something to eat. It was dim inside but I could see the tables and chairs were not clean. A few casual labourers were already there eating hot jellied bean curd. The restauranteur was a fat woman over forty, who looked weary and kept yawning because she had risen before sleep had satisfied her. She was not particularly enthusiastic when she saw me entering her restaurant as if the business did not matter much to her. I sat down at a table and asked her if she had soya-bean milk and deep-fried twisted dough sticks. She moved her swollen eyelids and answered listlessly: "No."

"Do you have rice porridge and crisp cakes?" I asked again. "Or egg custard will do."

"No—" she drawled.

"What do you have then?" I asked once more.

Not feeling like answering me, she just raised one of her strong arms and pointed to the few casual labourers eating by a table, meaning that what they were eating was all that she had.

The image of jellied bean curd, steamed bread, shelled peanuts and pickles appeared before my eyes. All of a sudden, I shouted in a deliberately loud voice: "Give me a bowl of jellied bean curd!"

The woman was given a start and rose to fetch the jellied bean curd for me. But just as she turned to go, I shouted again: "And a white flour steamed bread, too!"

The few casual labourers snickered.

The woman brought out a bowl of jellied bean curd and a white flour steamed bread and placed them heavily on the table before me. Then she leaned her body slantingly to look at me provocatively.

"Give me a dish of shelled peanuts and prickles!" I still shouted in a loud voice.

"I'm not deaf." The woman shook her body. "Why do you shout at me so loudly in an early morning like this? People coming to my restaurant are all my regular customers. Will you keep your voice down a bit?"

Pretending to hear nothing, I continued in a loud voice: "Was I speaking loudly? No, I couldn't have been. Did I frighten you?" I turned to ask the casual labourers, who then burst out laughing so hard as to splutter their white jellied bean curd.

The woman was back to her spirits and was not listless anymore when other customers entered the restaurant. I thought to myself: she looks like a true restauranteur now. And because I had a fit of shouting, I was back in my right mind too and finished eating up all the jellied bean curd and steamed bread in no

time at all. As for the dish of shelled peanuts, they were over-
stewed, their taste and colour were not good, which made me
think of the toes of the dead whenever I glanced at them, so I
didn't touch any of them.

Day had broken after I finished eating. I walked out of the
restaurant and found pedlars had appeared at all corners of the
street. Some hawked meat pies, some melons, fruits, sweets and
tea, and still others hot, stuffed steamed buns. I walked into the
bus station and bought a ticket in the ticket office before I went
to the long-distance bus. The driver was warming up the engine
with charcoal fire beneath the bus, and the young conductress
was shaking with cold because she wore far too little. I was the
first passenger on the bus. The window glass was covered with a
thick layer of frost. I scraped the frost off the glass with a fin-
gernail lightly, and without being aware, I scoured out the outline of a baby. The rays of the morning sun penetrated the crys-
tal scratches to come upon me, and the baby suddenly appeared,
golden, downy and lovable. Immediately it reminded me of
Luwei, and my eyes became moist with tears.

The long-distance bus reached Fish Pagoda at about nine thirty. I was the first passenger to get off. Like abandoning a
foundling, the bus dropped me at a crossroads far from the village and then sped on for Chutianba. After gazing around, I began to walk toward Fish Pagoda like a sheep seeking its lost
flock. The sky was pale, the sun was as wishy-washy as someone
suffering anaemia, and Fish Pagoda lay close by like a patch
sewn on the wilderness. I met neither man nor beast on my way.
Neither did I see any wisp of cooking smoke rising from the
chimneys when I entered the village. Only the old shepherd's
house wafted forth the smell of cooking smoke. The cow was

still standing beside the public conveniences with lowered head, its body still covered with frost. I quietly made for the vast open country. I very much wanted to see that mysterious shepherd.

In winter the sky was the same as the boundless wilderness in colour. There was no sharp contrast, no distinct demarcation between the sky and the earth, so the sky looked much lower, and the wilderness broader. In a glance, I spotted the dazzlingly dark figure, who was surrounded by the rolling white flock of sheep. Here was the shepherd.

I headed straight for him and the flock of sheep. My sudden intrusion turned the sheep into turmoil, and they flew into a fit of baaing.

The shepherd was much thinner and gloomier. He flicked his whip only once, and the sheep ran gaily forward.

"You came alone?" he asked hoarsely.

I nodded.

"Did you quarrel with him?" he asked again.

I shook my head.

"You're not fooling me." The shepherd felt uneasy. "You must have quarrelled with him. I can see it. But why did you quarrel?"

I had to tell him the truth: "Because of our son."

He drew a deep breath, opened his eyes wide and anxiously waited for me to go on.

"He was hungry after wakening up from his sleep. The nurse was a bit slow warming up milk for him, so he scratched the nurse's face and knocked the feeding bottle to the ground." I gazed at the shepherd's eyes. "I hit him."

"You hit your child?" the shepherd said lightly. "You hit him? You hit him at what part of his body?"

"His backside," I said. "You can't hit a child on its head, you know."

"That's right." The shepherd forced a bitter smile. "You can't hit a child's head."

"His father quarrelled with me because I hit our son." I spread out my two arms. "He never quarrelled with me before. He dotes on the child too much. We had a row last night."

"Children mustn't be spoilt." The shepherd cast a glance at me. "You can't say there's no truth in the saying 'dutiful sons come from under the club', but you can't punish a small child like yours either."

"I wanted to teach him to behave well while he's still small," I told him.

"Neither you nor your husband were wrong," he concluded after a long while. Then he asked: "Did you slip away secretly?"

"Yes," I told him. "I left home early in morning and came here on the long-distance bus to Chutianba."

"Your husband will come to take you back."

"No, I don't think so. He'd no idea I'd come here."

"He'll guess." His face broadened into a grin.

We walked on the grassland. As we walked along, he fixed his eyes at the flock of sheep in the distance, while I had my eyes on the white snow underfoot. When I asked him why he had failed to come to the place the previous Sunday, he answered with a sigh: "My daughter was seriously ill at home, I couldn't leave her."

"What's wrong with her?"

"She doesn't want to eat anything, and won't even drink water." The shepherd suddenly squatted down, put his whip away and held his head with two arms. "The doctor said she's become anorexic. She's so thin, she's like a shadow. I'm afraid she won't live long." Tears begans to fall.

"How old is she?"

"She's just in her sixth year," he said sobbingly.

"But how could she become anorexic?" I remembered that the American singer Karen Carpenter had died of such an illness.

"She wants..." he wailed. "She wants..."

"What can a little child like her have on her mind?" I said dubiously. "How is it possible?"

But he could only produce grievously the words: "She wants..."

"Anorexia is curable," I said. "Have you taken her to see a doctor in the city?"

"I've taken her wherever I thought fit. But nothing works. She refuses to eat or drink. She lives only on the glucose the doctor gives her." Suddenly, spreading his two arms wide, he looked at me with tears in his eyes. "She always wants..."

Not knowing how to comfort him, I only told him I would try to find an experienced doctor for his daughter in the city and asked if it would help if I went to his home to see the girl and try to talk to her in case I could help satisfy her needs.

"No one can satisfy her needs." He repeated: "She wants..."

"Does she want the moon in the sky?"

"She wants..." He mumbled the two words again.

His sorrow made me feel the weather was extraordinarily cold in the wilderness. The flock of sheep were now out of sight. A gust of wind sprang up and sent me shivering with cold. After a fit of tears, the shepherd calmed down. He gazed into the distance, saying, "Look!"

Scarcely had he finished the word when I heard the roaring of a car engine. A jeep was emerging from Fish Pagoda and running forward toward the wilderness.

"Wasn't I right?" the shepherd muttered. "But I must go and find my sheep." He bid goodbye to me and walked listlessly away in the direction of the village.

The jeep bumped along its way toward me, its wheels raising flurries of snow in all directions. I said to myself: Luwei's father has come to get me home, while tears started from my eyes.

The jeep halted. Yu Wei opened the door and popped out his head to squint at me smilingly: "Hey! One night we didn't share the same bed, and you feel wronged, eh?"

Thus said, he extended his two warm arms to me.

8. Silence

Luwei could waddle a few steps by supporting his hand on the wall. After he took a few more steps and did not fall down, he would turn back to mutter and mumble to us as if to cheer for his own success. If he was not careful enough and fell down, he would twitch his big mouth and cry until he was helped up. After Spring Festival, the weather became warmer with each passing day, and before people even became aware of it, the snow on the ground had begun to melt and the roads in the little lanes turned to mud. The sky turned blue, the white clouds became bright shrugging off the weight of winter, and branches of trees began to stretch out smoothly. In short, spring was silently creeping in.

It was one sunlit spring weekend that Auntie Lin brought back the news from her home that Sangsang had died. She had gone home to fetch clothes for the new season and found a letter in the pigeonhole from America. From the strange handwriting on the envelope Auntie Lin immediately sensed that someone must have written to tell her of Sangsang's death. With shaking hands, she opened the letter. It was from Sangsang's Chinese friend saying that Sangsang had died peacefully on a Sunday afternoon, a smile still hanging on her face when she breathed her last. Now she had been already buried. Before her death, her only wish was to drink a glass of sweet red wine, and she had had her wish fulfilled.

"She didn't change her bad habits and wanted to drink wine even when she died," Auntie Lin said shakingly.

"She didn't leave any word?" I asked.

"No," Auntie Lin replied. "She only asked her friend to tell me she died. She didn't leave a word."

"Sangsang was an immovable woman," I said. "Perhaps she didn't want you to feel sad for her."

"Death was a good thing for her," Auntie Lin said slowly. "Now I have no one to worry about in this world."

"Don't say it that way, Auntie Lin," I said. "You have Luwei. From now on you're one of our family."

Without saying another word, Auntie Lin turned for the kitchen. I quietly followed her and found her shedding tears while warming up milk for Luwei.

"After Yu Wei finishes his work, when it's warm, we'll go together to Fish Pagoda to sketch in the open country," I told her. "We'll take Luwei with us."

In the instant she nodded her head, a crowd of greyish clouds suddenly appeared before my eyes. That was the grey hair on Auntie Lin's head. For the first time I felt she had aged.

On a bright sunny Sunday at the end of April, we set off from the city early in the morning. Auntie Lin carried Luwei in her arms and Luwei held the wooden beads the shepherd had made for him. Wearing a snow-white woollen sweater and trousers, the boy looked to have all the energy of a mischievous lamb.

The sun had risen high after we drove out of the city. The bright sunlight was shining over the undulating land where all kinds of weeds and plants were turning green. The dynamic scene was pleasing to the eye and the mind. I could not help humming the American popular song *Yesterday Once More*. This nostalgic song often touched my heart. Its singer was the talented Karen Carpenter. It reminded of the shepherd, whom I had not seen for over a month, and I began to worry about his daughter.

"She's probably recovered," said Yu Wei, trying to dispel the worries from my mind. "We might come across the flock of sheep, the shepherd and his daughter."

"I hope so," I said.

Having stayed indoors for a whole winter, Luwei became very excited now sitting in the jeep and watching the changing scenes outside the window and kept up a lively stream of prattling. He had grown four snow-white teeth and could eat porridge and dried fish slices. His hair had become thick and dark after he had a haircut on the second day of the second month of the lunar year. He was now leaping and jumping joyfully in Auntie Lin's arms.

It was already the busy spring season, but there was no sign of seeds being sown in the fields in Fish Pagoda. It was unusually quiet when we entered the small village. No cooking smoke and not a soul were to be seen. What we saw were the plastic sheets before the windows which had become fragile and tattered after the weathering of a whole winter and which were now flapping in the spring breeze.

"Farmers don't work in the fields but stay at home, can they get rich by behaving like that?" Auntie Lin responded.

I felt very depressed. The decadent atmosphere in Fish Pagoda was so out of tune with the sunlit and enchanting scene of spring that had come upon the area around the village.

We drove past the old shepherd's house toward the vast land, which soon lay naked before us. We three adults were struck dumb by its beauty. Only Luwei was prattling nonstop by grasping Auntie Lin's hand when he set foot on the downy grass after getting out of the jeep. The grass had grown over an inch tall. Day lilies which are the first to know the arrival of spring, were blossoming here and there. In the far distance, near the bank of the river, a flock of sheep were moving slowly forward. Their fleeces were remarkably clean, so the flock appeared as white as snow. But the shepherd was not in sight; I felt lost and worried.

"Seems his daughter is not yet well," I said to Yu Wei.

"She's probably long been well," Yu Wei said to comfort me. "Perhaps he's got some urgent business and couldn't come today."

The flock of sheep moved gracefully like a broad puff of white cloud on the vast, early spring land.

Auntie Lin was unusually happy today. When she saw Luwei, now an eager toddler, fall to the ground and about to cry, she did not hasten over to pick him up as she usually did but pretended to fall down on the grass land with a cry herself. Looking at the agonised expression on her face, Luwei forgot his own situation and burst out chuckling.

Having asked Auntie Lin to take Luwei to play on the grass-land, Yu Wei and I went back to the old shepherd's home in Fish Pagoda to inquire about the shepherd.

The old man's granddaughter-in-law was tilling the land in her vegetable plot, her son playing beside her. When she saw us she greeted us warmly and led us into her house, pouring hot water for us and offering Yu Wei a cigarette.

The old shepherd, wearing a lined jacket, was sitting cross-legged on the edge of the *kang* smoking a pipe. While smoking, he coughed and grumbled that he was having an attack of tracheitis.

"Quit smoking then," Yu Wei said.

The old man curled his lips and swallowed a mouthful of saliva. "You can't stop when you've got the urge to smoke."

"It's like gambling," I joked.

The old man shrugged his shoulders without making any further response.

"Where is your grandson?" Yu Wei asked.

"He went to town to buy a kettle early this morning," the old man's granddaughter-in-law answered for him attentively. "The old kettle had been in use for over ten years. It leaked."

Then we asked the old man why his adopted son had not come and if the little girl had recovered from her anorexia. The old man raised his head to cast a sad glance at us and then turned back to smoke his pipe desperately.

I felt very tense.

The old man's granddaughter-in-law, dragging her son with her, went out to continue turning up the soil in the vegetable garden.

"He'll never come here to herd the sheep again," the old man said calmly. "And you'll never see him again."

"Is there anything wrong with him or his daughter?" I asked anxiously.

"His daughter died." The old man drew deeply at his pipe. "She was only six years old! It made our heart ache to have lost her."

"When did she die?" Yu Wei asked.

"A fortnight ago," the old man replied, "when the new grass had just begun to shoot."

"It happened so fast," I said. "He must be very sad." I remembered the shepherd's gloomy eyes. "He tried to tell me his daughter wanted something. What did she want so much that it made her develop anorexia?"

Putting down his pipe, the old man looked at us woodenly, his voice trembled: "She wanted her younger brother. She loved her younger brother. But her parents were forced to abandon him and someone took him away when he was seven months old. From that day on she refused to talk to her parents and to eat. All she wanted was her younger brother." Tears welled up the old man's eyes.

Panic-stricken, Yu Wei and I looked at one another, unable to utter a word.

"You should have realised, that adopted son of mine is Wang Jicheng from Bafangtai Village," the old man said with tears in his eyes. "When you went to his house to take the child, he hid outside the door and secretly wrote down the number of your jeep. He knew you'd never go back to Bafangtai again. So he came to me and told me that you loved to go for a drive in the country on Sundays. Bafangtai and Fish Pagoda are the two villages closest to the city. He predicted you would surely come to

Fish Pagoda. He told me the number of your jeep and asked me to keep an eye out for you."

I suddenly remembered how strangely the old man and his grandson had scrutinised our jeep's number plate.

"I hated him asking me to do such a thing, I knocked him on the head with my pipe," the old man continued. "But I still put a suggestion to him. For fear that you would guess who he was, I suggested he come to herd my flock of sheep on Sundays."

"But why did he want to see us?" I asked, bewildered.

"At the beginning he wanted to know how the child was getting along in the city, and whether you treated him well. If you treated the child well, he thought it would set his mind at rest." The old man picked up his pipe, filled the bowl with tobacco, lit it and, after wiping out the tears from his eyes, began to smoke. "But later, only when his daughter missed her younger brother so much she fell ill, did he begin to panic. He wanted to ask you to bring the child back once when he met you, but he couldn't bring himself to say it. The little girl might have got well if she had seen her younger brother again."

"But why didn't he tell me about it straightout?" I didn't know why I suddenly felt a sense of guilt taking a grip on me.

"He gave the child to you, how could his pride let him ask you for that?" the old man answered. "Sometimes he hoped you didn't like the child, so that he would have a reason to demand the child back. But you got along well with the child, and he had become your son. How could he tell you about it straightout?" The old man sighed deeply. "The poor little girl got thinner with each passing day. When she was to be buried after she died, I saw that her body was like a dry stalk of grass."

"Where was she buried?" Tears streamed down my cheeks as I

thought of that big-eyed little girl who had grabbed hold of my leg and bitten me for all she was worth. She lived for only six short years!

"She couldn't be buried close to her home," the old man said. "Or how could her family go on living?"

"She must have been buried in the wilderness beyond Fish Pagoda," I blurted out. "Right?"

The old man nodded his head. "But you won't be able to find the exact position of her tomb. Her father buried her very deeply with no grave mound. There was only a flat layer of earth on the top, which probably covered with grass by now. Even I couldn't find the place myself."

Tears kept rolling down my cheeks.

"You can set your mind at rest. Wang Jicheng won't come here again. He won't come to ask for information about the child anymore. He's a man who does what he says. You just go on raising the child well." The old man sighed again.

I fell silent. Yu Wei, while extending his hand to brush teardrops from my cheeks, kept shaking his head with grief. "Wang Jicheng asked me not to tell you about this," the old man continued in a low, deep voice. "But I had to tell you. You're reasonable people, you should know about it. I don't think you'll dislike the child all because of this." The old man sounded a bit worried.

"On the contrary," Yu Wei responded, "we'll love our son even more." He looked at the old man. "Because he has two families depending on him."

"I know you're kind-hearted people." Still with a worried look on his face, the old man asked: "Will you come to Fish Pagoda again?"

"Of course," I answered tearfully. "There are flocks of sheep here. What's more, there's Luwei's elder sister."

After bidding goodbye to the old man, we turned to go back to the green wilderness. The sun, hanging higher in the sky, was shining more brilliantly overhead. As we walked along, Yu Wei pulled my shoulders to him while I leaned closely over to him as though I were fearing the cold. Teardrops kept coming from my cheeks down to the lively grassland, to the glossy stalks of grass, to the beautiful flowers. In the far distance ahead, the flock of sheep was still moving forward like a large sheet of drifting cloud. I saw Auntie Lin and Luwei walking merrily around the flock of sheep.

Not a sound reached our ears as if silence reigned the entire vast land. I stopped, wanting to say a word to Yu Wei to express my love to him but could not bear to break the silence that had deeply touched my soul. I also wanted to say a word to the child who was running carefree ahead of us, but the distance between us was too great, and he would not hear me even if I shouted myself hoarse. Besides, the aloof tranquil atmosphere would not allow the slightest disturbance. However, with profound feeling, I still asked Luwei in the depth of my heart: "Please walk lightly, child. Don't hurt your elder sister with your steps!"

Christmas Eve, 1994, Harbin
Translated by Xiong Zhenru

Beloved Potatoes

"IF one day in July you look into the distance at Lizhen from the Milky Way, you will see a flower garden in full bloom. The flowers look like ears of grain, drooping like fuchsias, and tinted silver in the light of the stars and the moon. As you hold your breath and listen to the wind whistling gently over the garden, the eternal fragrance issuing from the otherwise mortal potato flowers will rise from the soil and penetrate your soul. Even from within Heaven's resplendent vault, this scene of the mundane world will never fail to move you to tears, which will fall on the fuchsia-shaped flowers and produce a melodic echo. Then you can console yourself with the thought that you tended these flowers with great attention in your previous life."

Such was the message the deceased members of Lizhen conveyed time and again to their potato-loving fellow villagers through their dreams. Thus newly awakened from their dreams, people who had come to till the potato fields would converse with each other like this:

"Last night, my son's grandpa said that he wanted terribly to eat potatoes in the nether world now. Why is he so eager while the potatoes are still only in bloom?"

"Lao Xin said the same. He complained that I hadn't planted enough potatoes for him to smell the fragrance from our fields. How is it that he's still so sensitive to smell?"

The potato flowers would all listen to their conversation.

Every family in Lizhen grew potatoes. Qin Shan and his wife were the village's leading potato growers, tilling a total of three *mu* on the southern slope. Bags of potatoes had to be planted in the field in spring and when the potatoes flowered in summer, the Qins' field was the most colourful, in mixed hues of purple, pink and white. In autumn the Qins naturally harvested more potatoes than anyone else. In late autumn they sold the potatoes in town, and saved up the money. The surplus was kept for the next year's seedcrop and shared by humans and animals as food.

Qin Shan was a skinny and swarthy man who always went barefooted in summer. His wife, Li Aijie, was half a head taller. Though she was not pretty she was fair skinned, gentle and virtuous. The couple always went to the potato field together, with their nine-year-old daughter Fenping in tow, picking potato flowers, catching locusts and teasing the meek and mute cow with a willow rod. Qin Shan was an inveterate smoker who was often seen puffing at a cigarette his eyes narrowed in a most contented fashion. He grew lot of tobacco in his vegetable garden. When the tobacco leaves were ripe in autumn, he would tie them into fan-shaped bundles and suspend them from under the eaves of the house like so many ancient-looking chimes swaying gently in the autumn wind. When winter came, Qin Shan would sit on his *kang** chain-smoking; occasionally he invited friends

---

* *Kang* is a heatable brick bed common in peasant homes in north China.

to share his tobacco. His teeth and fingers were baked yellow with nicotine and his lips were the colour of pig liver. His smoking habit was a constant source of discord between him and his wife.

Due to the amount of cigarettes he consumed, Qin Shan coughed a lot, especially in spring and autumn, and particularly at night. Li Aijie often complained to neighbouring women that she had to wash her head every other day, or the smell of the tobacco in her hair would make her sick. Her listners would tease her, saying it must be that you are always in Qin Shan's arms while he smokes. Li Aijie would flush and retort, "Nonsense, Qin Shan is not that romantic."

Who could tell if Qin Shan was romantic or not?

Qin Shan and his wife loved to eat potatoes. So did their daughter. There were infinite ways of making potato dishes in Qin Shan's family; steamed, boiled, baked, stewed, fried, or in soup. In winter Fenping often baked whole potatoes on the second shelf of the stove and ate them as desert.

In Lizhen potatoes came in season toward the end of July. Children would steal into the field on the southern slope and searched for finger-wide cracks on the ridges. They would surely come by some plump potatoes if their fingers reached far enough into the cracks. They put the potatoes in small baskets and carried them home to be cooked with kidney beans. This dish was considered a rare delicacy. Of course, when the cracks in their own field had been explored and no premature potatoes could be seen, they would steal like little foxes into Qin Shan's potato field, always on the alert lest they should be noticed by Qin Shan arriving to work in his field. Qin Shan actually did not care about those few potatoes that disappeared with the children. As he approached the field, he would first cough loudly to warn the children so as not to frighten them and give them the chance to run away. The children thought themselves very clever and told their parents when they returned home, "Smoking makes Qin Shan cough so bad that he even coughs in the potato field."

Early one autumn, while he was munching happily on potatoes Qin Shan began to cough, his shoulders trembling violently like a coat-hanger rattling in a strong wind. He felt that the vital organs of his body were being completely jolted out of place, and he was very uncomfortable. Li Aijie complained as she pounded his back, "You keep on smoking, smoking. I'm going to burn your tobacco leaves tomorrow!"

Qin Shan instinctively made to fight back; however, he did not have the strength. That night he continued to cough seriously and felt sick. His coughing woke Fenping, who slept by the door. "Pa, shall I bring you some radish to help your cough?" she asked.

"No, Fenping. Go back to sleep," replied Qin Shan as he pounded his chest.

Qin Shan was eventually exhausted by his coughing and fell asleep. Li Aijie was worried about her husband and woke up early the next morning. She turned her head to Qin Shan and was shocked to see some blood stains on his pillow. Her first thought was to wake her husband and show him the blood. But on second thoughts, she decided it was no good for people to lose blood. If Qin Shan knew that he had coughed up blood, wouldn't he feel worse? She slightly lifted Qin Shan's head, removed the pillow and put her own under his head instead. Qin Shan was vaguely disturbed, but he immediately resumed his sleep. He was tired after his long and hard fits of coughing the night before.

Li Aijie got up quickly and washed the pillow. When Qin Shan rose, she filled a bowl with porridge and said to him, "Let's go and see the doctor in town. Your coughing is really serious."

"I'll be OK if I stop smoking for a few days. No need to see the doctor," said Qin Shan, his face as pale as cement.

"How can you be cured without seeing the doctor? If you don't see a doctor it will only get worse."

"Coughing won't kill me," Qin replied. "If anybody goes to town ask them to bring me two *jin* of pears and I'll be fine."

Li Aijie thought to herself, "Coughing won't kill people. But if you start splitting blood trouble is sure to follow behind." She was thinking this as she handed Qin Shan the bowl of porridge and her hands trembled. She didn't dare to look into Qin Shan's eyes. She decided she should just talk as if nothing had happened. "What a nice day! So cloudless!"

Qin Shan nodded his head by way of reply while he drank his porridge.

"Lao Zhou's pig refuses to eat anything these days. Lao Zhou's wife is so worried that she's been running around looking for a vet to give the pig an injection. Tell me how the pig could be sick, since autumn is already here?" Li asked.

"Aren't pigs the same as people? They can get sick any time." Qin Shan put down his porridge bowl as he replied.

"You only ate half?" Li ventured in a disappointed voice. "I washed the millet three times so there isn't a single husk left. It should taste wonderful!"

"I don't feel like eating," Qin Shan answered, coughing slightly. Hearing Qin Shan resume his coughing so early in the day made Li Aijie feel more nervous and frightened.

After breakfast, Li continued to urge him to go to the hospital. She pleaded repeatedly until he agreed. It was thus that Qin Shan and his wife went off to town on Fei Xili's horse cart. They sat at the back of the cart. It had just rained and the road was muddy so their legs were spattered with mud as the cart wheels rolled on. "Better there's not so much rain this autumn, otherwise, we'll be rolling in mud when time for the potato harvest comes," Li Aijie said.

Fei Xili cracked the whip and turned his head, "Only your family is afraid of autumn rain. Why do you grow so many potatoes? You must have quite a stash of money by now. You can probably afford fifty horses, right?"

Qin Shan smiled and said, "I don't have even one horse."

"It's OK, I'm not going to your stable and make off with your horse, you don't have to worry about that. Come on, tell me the truth," said Fei Xili.

Li Aijie interrupted, "Please stop teasing my Qin Shan. If he had earned that much money by selling potatoes, he would have taken a young girl as his concubine."

Fei Xili burst into laughter and the horse started to trot happily. The cart bumped and the bell below the horse's neck jingled.

"I've never had the idea of taking a concubine," Qin Shan retorted, "I'm not a landlord."

"What if you were a landlord?" Li Aijie asked.

"I would marry only you. First wife is what I loved." Qin Shan turned his head and spat on the road. "You can marry a young guy with the money from potatoes after I'm gone. I'm sure you'll have a better life." Li Aijie almost cried on hearing him joke this way.

The doctor made an X-ray of Qin Shan's chest and told him to come back again. Three days later, Qin Shan and his wife once again rode Fei Xili's town-bound cart to the hospital. The doctor told Li Aijie secretly, "Your husband has three tumours in his lungs and one of them is already quite large. I'd advise you to take him to Harbin for further examinations."

"Could it be cancer?" Li Aijie asked in a low voice, deeply worried.

"We can't say definitely one way or the other at this point," the doctor replied. "The tumour might well be malignant. The medical facilities here are very limited and we aren't able to make a definite diagnosis. Your husband is still young so I suggest you get him to a better hospital for further examinations as soon as possible."

"He is only thirty-six," Li Aijie said sadly, "and this is his birth year*."

"A person's birth year is always troublesome," the doctor said sympathetically.

The couple bought some pears back with them to Lizhen. Fenping was very happy to see her parents back home and thought her father was well. She rushed to snatch the pears from him. Qin Shan stopped coughing and was very tender to his wife that night, but the respite may just have been due to the cooling effect of the pears. Li Aijie found herself in a great dilemma. She was worried that sex might make her husband worse. But she was also reluctant to spurn his advances because she was afraid that such opportunities might become fewer and fewer in the future. She felt totally helpless and uncomfortable. Moreover, she

---

* In China, the birth year is related to the Twelve Terrestrial Branches; the recurrent year in the cycle is considered troublesome.

found herself embarrassed and responded with reluctance. Qin Shan couldn't help complaining, "What's wrong with you tonight?"

Li Aijie woke early the next morning and looked at Qin Shan's pillow in the soft morning light. The pillow was clean and there was not a drop of blood on it. She was consoled to a certain degree, thinking to herself that what the doctor said might not be absolutely correct and one should not believe it all. Moreover, they could attend to their affairs as usual, like weeding the potato fields, sprinkling fertiliser on the cabbages and making braids of garlic to hang on the gables. But it didn't last long. One week later Qin Shan began to cough seriously again and this time he saw the blood for himself. His face became sallow and he was struck dumb.

"Let's go to Harbin and try some other doctors," Li Aijie suggested, deeply grieved.

"It's no good sign for a man to cough blood," Qin Shan said. "I'm going to die sooner or later so why waste a lot of money trying to cure my disease."

"But if you are sick you should at least try and cure yourself," Li Aijie replied. "All diseases can be cured in big cities. Since we've never been to Harbin, it might be worth our while to go and take a look."

Qin Shan became silent. The couple talked it over for half the night and finally decided to go to Harbin. Li Aijie took all of their five thousand yuan savings with her, asking their neighbour to take care of Fenping, the pig and a couple of chickens. The neighbour asked them if they could try and be back before autumn harvest. Qin Shan smiled and said, "Even if I have only one breath left, I'll use it to come back alive and reap my last potatoes."

Li Aijie patted Qin Shan's shoulder and said, "Nonsense!"

The couple hitched a ride on Fei Xili's cart, this time going to town to sell vegetables. Seeing that Qin Shan was in low spirits, Fei Xili said, "If you trust me, don't go and see doctors. You'll be fine if you just smoke less and take more exercise."

"I work in the potato field every day. Don't I get enough exercise?" Qin Shan smiled drily and continued, "Damn disease! I'm going to the big city with my wife to have a look. I'll buy her a pair of leather shoes and a cheongsam with a long slit in the sides."

"I won't wear such a dress and shame your good name," Li Aijie mumbled.

They bought half a kilo of pancakes and two packets of pickles and headed for the railway station. The ticket fare was not as expensive as they imagined. When they got on the train they were very happy to find two seats next to each other. On their way Li Aijie kept aahing and oohing over the sights out of the window:

"Look at those purple flowers! How beautiful!"

"Look at those stout cattle! Whose are they?"

"See that family! They must be very rich. They even painted their gate blue."

"Is that man with a straw hat on like Wang Fu of our village? But Wang Fu is a bit more robust."

Qin Shan's wife's chatter reminded him of her younger days, and a strong sense of sadness, a sadness as intense as the evening glow, struck him. "If I am not that sick," he thought to himself, "I'll be able to hear more of her sweet voice. If I am fated to die, that sweet voice will vanish like a flash. If so, who will embrace her warm and smooth body, who will help her take care of Fenping, and who will tend that large piece of potato field?"

Qin Shan dared not let his imagination run on further.

Arriving at Harbin, they had no interest in seeing the city. They first ate some jellied bean curd and fried twisted dough sticks at the railway station and then asked how to get to the hospital. A cook with a white apron on recommended several hospitals to them and told them how to get there by bus.

"You recommended so many hospitals, but which one is the cheapest?" Qin Shan asked.

Li Aijie looked at Qin Shan hard and said, "We want to go to the best hospital. We don't care how expensive it is."

The cook was a warm-hearted person and gave his opinion about the conditions of each hospital, finally choosing one for them.

It took them much trouble to get to that hospital. Qin Shan was hospitalised immediately. Li Aijie first had to put down a deposit of eight hundred yuan, after which she went to buy daily necessities to be used in the hospital like lunch box, spoon, cup, towel and slippers. Qin Shan shared a ward with seven patients, two of whom were on oxygen. The sounds of coughing, spitting and water-drinking accompanied the irregular breathing of the dying. The doctor told Li Aijie that Qin Shan needed a CT examination which was to be very expensive, but she was determined to go ahead whatever the cost.

Qin Shan's face turned pale and wan after he entered the hospital. He felt he was falling into a big trap, especially when he found that his fellow patients were all in low spirits. Li Aijie bought back two tea-boiled eggs and some bread for supper. The patient next to Qin Shan was a middle-aged man who was very fat. With an ice pillow under his head, the patient was eating supper with the help of his wife. It seemed that he was suffering from apoplexy, for his mouth was somewhat askew and couldn't speak properly. It was hard for him to eat. The woman who helped him was around thirty, short-haired, wan and sallow. The woman inadvertently spilt a spoonful of soup on his neck, and the patient was so irritated that he knocked the spoon away and cursed, "Bitch! Demon!" The woman put down the soup bowl and rushed out to the hall heart-broken.

Having finished their meal, Li Aijie and Qin Shan asked the others where to order meals and get boiled water. The people answered their questions warmly. It was dusk when Li Aijie came out of the ward with a thermos in her hand. The dark hall smelt gloomy and terrible. It was here that she ran across the woman who had been scolded by her husband. She was standing by a pile of coal beside the tea-house, smoking. On seeing Li Aijie she asked:

"What's wrong with your husband?"

"He's not been diagnosed yet. Tomorrow he'll have CT scan," Li Aijie said.

"What's his problem?"

"His lungs," Li Aijie said as she turned on the tap and listened to the sound of the water flowing into the thermos. "He even vomitted blood."

"Really?" The woman was startled, and sighed deeply.

"Your husband has apoplexy?" Li Aijie asked with deep concern.

"Yes. It's also called cerebral haemorrhage. He almost died. When the doctors finally got to him, he had lost feeling on one side of his body and could no longer move. Since then he has become more and more irritable. I'm the victim once he gets even slightly irritated. You've seen it," the woman complained.

"Sick people are usually anxious and worried," Li Aijie consoled her as she rose, putting the cork in the thermos. "You need to be patient with him."

"It's really bad luck to have a sick husband." The woman stubbed out her cigarette. "Where are you from?"

"Lizhen," Li Aijie said. "It's two whole days' ride by train."

"So far away," the woman said. "I'm from Mingshui. The one who was in your husband's bed before, died last night. He was only forty-two. He died of liver cancer, leaving behind two children and his mother who is almost eighty. His wife cried so bitterly."

Holding the thermos Li Aijie's arm suddenly felt like jelly. She asked in a low voice, "Do you think lung cancer is curable?"

"I don't like to dampen hope, but cancer is really incurable," the woman said. "It's more worthwhile to spend the money on sightseeing instead of on doctors and medicine. But you don't have to worry too much now. Your husband might not have cancer at all. He's not been finally diagnosed yet, has he!"

Li Aijie felt more disappointed. Her legs became like jelly too and her eyes lost their focus.

"Do you have any relatives in Harbin?" the woman inquired.

"No," Li Aijie replied.

"Where will you spend the night?"

"I'll just stay by my husband and keep him company."

"Don't you know that the patient's relatives are not allowed to stay at the ward unless the patient's condition is critical? It seems to me that you're not up to living in a hotel. Why don't you come to stay with me. You only need to pay a hundred yuan for a whole month."

"What kind of place is it?" Li Aijie asked.

"It's not very far from the hospital, only twenty minutes' walk, among a group of low houses that are to be knocked down. The owners of the house are an old couple. They have a ten-square-metre room they let. I lived with the woman whose husband died of liver cancer for some time. She went home after her husband died."

"It's so kind of you," Li Aijie said.

"My name is Wang Qiuping," the woman said. "Just call me Sister Ping."

"Sister Ping," Li Aijie said, "my daughter's name is also Ping, Fenping."

They left the tea-house across the pavement covered with coal cinders and went back through the hallway to the ward area. They walked one after the other and their steps were very heavy. The patients' relatives walked to and fro across this area to fetch water and throw away leftovers. The garbage can in the toilet smelt terribly.

When Li Aijie was about to leave him and go back with Wang Qiuping, Qin Shan suddenly grabbed her hand and said, "Aijie, if this is diagnosed to be cancer, we won't stay to suffer here. I'd rather die in our potato field in Lizhen."

"You're talking nonsense." Li Aijie, her face flushed, eased her hand out of Qin Shan's. Wang Qiuping was watching.

"You don't have to worry about me. Eat good and rest well," Qin Shan said to his wife.

"OK," Li Aijie replied.

The owner of the house was very happy when she saw that

Wang Qiuping had brought her a new tenant. The old lady quickly went about boiling a kettle of water and washed two cucumbers for them to eat. The room was small and the two beds were constructed of bricks supporting wood planks. Between the two beds was a short rectangular table painted in many colours. On the table were tooth brushes, mirrors, tea-cups and toilet paper. Several worn-out clothes hung on the wall. Behind the door was a chamber pot with a wooden cover. All these appeared more dim and gloomy under a low-watt light.

Having washed their feet, Wang Qiuping and Li Aijie turned off the light. As they lay there in the darkness they started to talk:

"I felt so envious of you when I saw your husband grab your hand," Wang Qiuping said. "You're so much in love."

"That's why I felt almost as ill as he did after he became sick," said Li Aijie in a low voice.

"My husband and I had never had such feelings for each other even before he became sick. We quarrelled very frequently. I have done what I can faithfully since he became sick, but he gets more and more easily irritated. I've been waiting on him for three months and there's been no improvement. Our money's all spent, we've had to borrow a large amount. I'm so worried that I even thought of committing suicide. My two children are still so young and my mother-in-law is fat and lazy, and fond of making oblique accusations."

"Do you farm too?" asked Li Aijie.

"Yes, we are farmers. He started an oil mill with another man the year before last and made several thousand yuan, but he lost the money in the gambling house."

"How are you going to pay your debt?"

"I'm beginning to find small jobs," said Wang Qiuping. "At three o'clock each morning, I would go to the booking office in the railway station to line up for sleeper tickets. The ticket dealer pays me fifteen yuan for them. At noon, I go to restaurants to collect leftovers for a pig farm and I earn eight or ten yuan. I can make twenty or so to save a day."

"Does your husband know what you're going through for him?"

"I would be happy if he would stop finding fault with me. I never expected that he would love me," Wang Qiuping sighed. "If he doesn't recover and remains paralysed, the rest of my life will be really hard. Sometimes I really wish he would..."

Li Aijie knew what she was going to say and was astounded.

"If you were me, you'd understand," Wang said wearily. "If your husband has cancer, you'll need a large sum of money, but money won't necessarily cure him. However, I'll help get you some work, like selling lunch-boxes, baby-sitting and sending milk..."

Wang Qiuping's voice became fainter and fainter. Fatigue finally overcame her and soon she was asleep. Li Aijie remained awake and restless, at one moment wondering if Qin Shan could sleep well in the hospital and at another wondering if Fenping had adapted herself to the neighbour's house. She thought too about the potato field on the south slope of Lizhen. At last, when she was very tired she went off to sleep. It was bright day when she woke up the next morning. The owner of the house was sweeping the courtyard. Some grey doves were cuckooing on the window sill. Wang Qiuping had already gone out to work.

"Did you sleep well?" the owner of the house asked warmly.

"Very well," Li replied. "All my tiredness is gone."

The owner of the house asked Li Aijie questions as she busied around, like "What's your husband suffering from? How many people are there in your family? How many rooms does your house have?" She told Li Aijie that Wang Qiuping had gone to the railway station early in the morning to line up for the sleeper tickets. "Wang asked me to tell you to go and buy yourself a snack around the corner of the street when you got up," she said.

Having washed her face, Li Aijie went to the hospital reversing the same route she had taken the night before. There were so many cars and pedestrians on the streets that she felt she could never count them clearly in a lifetime. She decided that the roads in the town were miserable and overloaded. It was cloudy, but most women were wearing skirts and dresses, with their legs exposed. They all had exquisite and delicate leather bags on their shoulders and their high-heels struck the road loudly. She had intended to buy a snack for breakfast around the corner of the street as her landlady suggested, but she directly went to the hospital with her stomach empty, because she was very much worried about Qin Shan. The moment she entered the hall, she saw the door of Qin Shan's ward pushed open. Five or six people came out, among whom were doctors and strangers. Behind them a patient was being wheeled out. Li Aijie was so frightened that her legs threatened to give way under her. Her relief when she realised that the patient was not Qin Shan was enormous.

Qin Shan had ordered millet porridge for his wife. He covered it very tightly for fear that it might get cold, putting it on his stomach, holding it in his hand. When Li Aijie came in, he took the box out from under his quilt smilingly and said, "It's still warm. Come quick and eat it."

Li Aijie was on the verge of tears and asked in a low voice, "Did you cough in the night?"

Qin Shan winked at her and shook his head, saying, "I couldn't sleep soundly without you beside me."

Li Aijie looked at Qin Shan, her eyes moistened. Then she lowered her head and started to eat the bowl of porridge. Outside the window leaves rustled in the wind. The rustling reminded her of the sound of the wheat straw Qin Shan used to tickle her ear when they were young. Li Aijie took a look at Wang Qiuping's husband, lying paralysed on the bed, his head tilted to one side. As she watched, the sick man gulped down a fried pancake greedily, his facial expression like that of an innocent child.

The result of Qin Shan's examination came out soon. Li Aijie had the feeling that everything was finished when she was called to the doctor's office.

"He is already in the late stage of lung cancer. It has spread beyond containment," the doctor told her.

Li Aijie remained silent. She only felt that she had suddenly dropped into a dark well, denied all presence of sunshine.

"It is unlikely that an operation will be effective," the doctor said. "You must think it over. He may first take some medicine, but better not let him know the truth, otherwise it will affect him psychologically."

Li Aijie came out of the doctor's office on leaden legs. The world suddenly became alien to her, though the hallway leading to the ward was full of people. She came to the flower garden in front of the admission office and wished that she could cry before the carefree flowers and grass. But her tears were held back by the tremendous sorrow in her heart. Only then did she realise that people in despair had no tears at all.

In order to conceal her mental turmoil, Li Aijie stealthily picked a flower in the garden and hid it up her sleeve before going back to her husband. Qin Shan was drinking water. The bright sunlight clung to the contour of his thin pale cheeks. His lips were dry and chapped. Li Aijie took out the flower while Qin Shan was off guard and said, "Smell it. Is it fragrant?" She held the flower up to his nose as she said this.

Qin Shan smelt it hard and said, "Not as fragrant as potato flowers."

"Potato flowers have no fragrance," Li Aijie corrected him.

"Who said potato flowers have no fragrance? Potato flowers' fragrance is special. Usually people are unable to smell it. But once they do, they never forget it." Qin Shan looked around and found that nobody was paying any attention to what he was saying, so he teased her boldly by saying, "Just like the smell of your body."

Li Aijie smiled bitterly. Then she added as if she was very happy, "You know why I stole a flower for you? We need to have a celebration. The doctors have diagnosed that you only have a very common lung disease and a couple of months' injection will cure it."

"Did the doctor tell you so?" Qin Shan asked, down-hearted, as if he knew what she meant.

"The doctor told me a moment ago. You may go and ask him if you don't believe me," Li Aijie said.

"It's good that I have no dangerous disease. I needn't go and ask about it," Qin Shan said. "We've been here for over a week and it's now time to reap our potatoes."

"Hold your horses. There are many kind-hearted people in Lizhen and they won't leave our potatoes to rot in the field," Li Aijie replied.

"It's important to reap what one sowed," Qin Shan said, then changed the topic suddenly. "You keep hold of our money, but can you give me a little to spend?"

"I'll give you however much you want," Li Aijie smiled and said. "You're now lying in the hospital and unable to go out shopping. What's the use of having money?"

"To order some delicious food or to buy some fruit," Qin Shan said as he took up his cup and drank some water. "Moreover, I'll feel better if I have money on me."

Li Aijie took three hundred yuan from her pocket and gave it to Qin Shan.

That same afternoon the nurse gave Qin Shan his first infusion. Li Aijie talked to him as the infusion liquid flowed from an unlabelled bottle.

Dusk had arrived when the infusion was done. The meal they ordered, rice with a soy bean dish, came. Though he didn't eat much, Qin Shan seemed to be in high spirits, for all the while he chatted on glibly.

It was dusk when Wang Qiuping brought a meal to her husband. They were shocked to see her eye sockets black and her hands bandaged. Wang Qiuping's luck had began to forsake her these days. The railway officials had taken stern measures against ticket scalpers and they'd all disappeared. She thought she could buy tickets herself and then sell them at a higher price, but she got up very late these days, and therefore she often failed to get any tickets at all. To make the matter worse, she had injured her hand on the iron railing. Bad-tempered as her husband was, he had an unusual appetite, wanting to eat chicken and fish almost everyday. Wang Qiuping had no choice but to comply.

"Qin Shan, would you like to have some chicken soup too?" asked Wang Qiuping.

"No, thank you. Aijie and I have just eaten," Qin Shan replied, smilingly.

Wang Qiuping's husband gave her an angry look and said, "You think he is younger than I and asked him to have chicken soup. What, are you trying to seduce him!"

Wang Qiuping shook her head and sighed as she fed her husband one spoonful after another. After feeding her husband, Wang Qiuping suddenly said to Li Aijie on their way to the toilet, "So many nice people who should not die have passed away, but he who should die is still alive to torture me. Sometimes I really feel like poisoning him."

Looking into Wang Qiuping's eyes blankly, Li Aijie said, "Qin Shan has been finally diagnosed." She flung herself into Wang Qiuping's arms and burst into tears. "I'm more unfortunate than you are. He won't be able to give me the opportunity to be tortured any more!"

The two women held each other and cried.

That night, Li Aijie and Wang Qiuping stayed awake almost until dawn. They bought a bottle of liquor, got drunk and continued to shed tears. In the beginning they felt dizzy but strangely enough, when they had cried until they could cry no more, they became sombre-minded and no longer felt sleepy. They started to tell family stories, talking till dawn when they finally felt drowsy. In the splendour of the dawn, they succumbed to deep sleep.

Li Aijie dreamed that when she and Qin Shan were passing a grassland on their way to weeding the potato field, Qin Shan fell into the marshland while picking a flower for her. Seeing Qin Shan falling deeper and deeper in the quagmire, Li Aijie was so worried that she cried out loudly in her dream. She rubbed her temples as she looked at the empty liquor bottle, and the left-overs of sausage, dried bean curd and peanuts on the table. She remembered drinking with Wang Qiuping who was still sleeping soundly under a thin woollen blanket, her hair hanging down loosely and her nostrils flaring rhythmically. Wang Qiuping looked much prettier now. Li Aijie grabbed her watch and found it was already high noon. Greatly agitated, she pushed Wang to wake her up saying, "Sister Ping, it's noon. We should be at the hospital."

With effort Wang Qiuping sat up and rubbed her eyes with the back of her hands. She complained sadly, "I've missed my chance to line up for the tickets and collect the pig feed. She straightened her clothes and then suddenly lay down on the bed, resigning herself to the will of Heaven. "It's already noon," she said. "Better sleep on till evening and save a meal."

Li Aijie knew that she was just releasing her anger when she said that. By the time Li Aijie had finished washing and re-turned to the room, as expected Wang Qiuping had got up. She told Li that she had decided to go back to Mingshui in a couple of days, for she dreamed that her children had been bitten by a dog. "One child was bitten on the arm, the other on the leg. They fell into my arms and cried and cried. They are so unlucky to have been born into my family."

"Dreams are supposed to be interpreted the other way around," Li Aijie consoled her. "If you dreamed that they were crying they must really be smiling."

"I miss my children," again Wang Qiuping sighed. "It's autumn harvest season. I can't always rely on my mother's family for help."

"It's time for harvest and my family has a large potato field," Li Aijie said with a strong sense of loss and sadness as if autumn had passed before she knew it and her feet had suddenly stepped on thin ice.

As they talked they came out to the street, and each bought a thin pancake and started to eat, leaning against a fence thick with dust. The shining sun caused them to narrow their eyes as they lazily watched the passers-by, traffic, posters on the street and listened to the car speakers, the pop songs the tape recorder was playing in front of the music cassette stand and the pedlars' repeated hawking of their wares.

It was pastlunch time when they got to the hospital. Li Aijie was stunned the moment she entered the ward, for Qin Shan had disappeared. His hospital clothes were on the bed, and the lunch-box and other things on the bedside cupboard were there no more.

A nurse was giving an injection to a patient. When she saw Li Aijie, she said to her harshly, "Relative of bed No. 5, how is it that your husband has disappeared?"

"He was here when I left him last night. How could he leave the hospital?" Li Aijie replied angrily. "I should be asking you where he has gone!"

"The hospital is not a nursery," the nurse retorted. "Is your husband staying in this hospital or not? If not, there's a whole lot right there waiting for his bed."

Li Aijie lifted Qin Shan's bed sheet and found that his slippers were missing. Then she sat on the bed and started to cry. The patient next to Qin's bed said that Qin Shan was well the night before but around four o'clock in the morning when it was still dark, Qin Shan got up and left. He had just thought that Qin had gone to the toilet.

"Is Qin Shan going to die?" Li Aijie thought to herself. "Wang Qiuping and I cried in the toilet yesterday. Although I washed my face many times and stayed in the courtyard for a long time to calm myself down in the breeze, he might have noticed some trace of my swollen red eyes. He has gone without saying goodbye. It seems that he has decided to end his life."

Wang Qiuping left her husband and hurried to join Li Aijie in her search for Qin Shan. They went to the banks of the Songhuajiang River, the railway crossroads by Jihong Bridge, the deep woods in the parks and all the other places that might attract potential suicides. However, nobody had jumped into the river, thrown himself on the rails or hanged himself on trees in the parks. It got dark. They still could not find Qin Shan. What they could see was an endless stream of strangers hurrying home. Li Aijie leaned on the iron fence of Jihong Bridge and began to cry.

They thought hard where Qin Shan might have gone. Finally Wang Qiuping suggested that he might have gone to the Immortal Temple to live out his days as a monk. Li Aijie thought it was reasonable. Maybe Qin Shan had it in his mind that his disease might be cured and his soul saved if he gave himself up to Buddhism. After a sleepless night they headed for the Immortal Temple early the next morning. They came to the head monk and asked if any one had recently presented himself to be a monk. The abbot put his hands together, murmured "Buddha bless me," and then shook his head slightly. Then they made straight for the Catholic church and Christian church on the main street. Why the churches? Maybe, they thought, churches were homes lost souls. They searched for Qin Shan right through to the afternoon but could not find a hint of him anywhere. Then they went back to the place where they lived and began to watch the house-owner's television set to see if there was any news about a lost man or if there had been any unusual accidents. Unfortunately, they got no information from the television.

It was not until two o'clock in the afternoon that it occurred to a worried Li Aijie that Qin Shan must have gone back to Lizhen. How was it possible that a man who intended to commit suicide would take away his lunch-box, towels, slippers and other odds and ends? Li also remembered that Qin Shan had asked money from her the other day. All these confirmed in her mind the fact that Qin Shan had gone home. She started to pack at once.

"Sister Ping, please can you help me with the release formalities at the hospital," Li Aijie said without raising her head. "Qin Shan must have gone back home."

"Isn't he going to stay in the hospital to get treatment?" Wang Qiuping shouted.

"He must have understood that his disease was incurable and he will not accept treatment for an incurable disease," Li Aijie sobbed as she said this. "He is going to leave the money to me and Fenping. I know his intention."

"How was it possible that you got such a kind-hearted man?" Wang Qiuping sobbed. "How was it that he went back home without you?"

"How could I let him go if he asked me to go back home with him?" Li Aijie said. "It's now too late to catch today's train. I'll have to hurry back tomorrow."

Once she was clear about Qin Shan's whereabouts, Li Aijie calmed down. In the afternoon, Wang Qiuping accompanied her to deal with formalities at the hospital. The hospital did not a-gree to return her deposit at first, saying that the patient had been treated in the hospital for over a week and had taken a sub-stantial amount of medicine. Unable to persuade them, Li Aijie went to Qin Shan's doctor for help. Aware of the details, the doctor helped Li Aijie get refunded for what was left of the de-posit.

At night, Li Aijie unpacked her luggage, took out a pair of new woollen trousers and handed them to Wang Qiuping, say-ing, "Sister Ping, I made them three years ago but I've only worn them a couple of times. City people tend to judge people only by their appearances, so you may wear them when you go out on business. You're a bit taller than I and you may have to let down the hem."

Holding the pair of trousers in her hands, Wang Qiuping cried and her tears dissolved into the woollen fabric.

It was autumn harvest season when Li Aijie reached home. Every family was digging potatoes in the field on the south slope. It was afternoon and the sky was clear and bright without a hint of a cloud. The cool wind was blowing in the lanes. Li Aijie didn't go home but headed straight for the potato field on the south slope instead. On her way there, she saw many hand-carts on the edges of the fields. People in the fields were dig-ging, picking potatoes, and putting them into bags. A neighbour's dog caught sight of her and came to rub her trouser legs with its muzzle, its tail wagging, as if saying "Hello, so you're back."

Li Aijie could see Qin Shan digging potatoes in the distance. Fenping was picking potatoes behind him, a basket in her hand. He was dressed in a blue cloth jacket and the heavy afternoon sunshine fell on him, making him shine brightly. Li Aijie called out from the bottom of her heart, "Qin Shan..." and her cheeks were burned by her own tears.

The Qins settled down for a leisurely winter after all the potatoes had been gathered in. Qin Shan was becoming rapidly thinner and thinner until he could hardly eat a thing. He often stared at Li Aijie affectionately without saying a word. In calmness Li Aijie went about cooking, washing clothes, making the bed and sleeping with him. One evening, when snow fell and Fenping was roasting potato slices on the stove, Qin Shan said to Li Aijie, "I bought you something when I came back from Harbin. Guess what it is."

"How can I guess?" Li Aijie's heart throbbed strongly.

Qin Shan got off the *kang* and took out a red paper parcel from the chest. Softly, he unwrapped layer after layer of the paper, and there appeared a diamond blue silk cheongsam, which emitted a dazzling sheen in the electric light.

"Oh!" Li Aijie exclaimed with surprise.

"Isn't it beautiful?" asked Qin Shan. "You may wear it next summer."

"Next summer..." Li Aijie said sadly. "I'll wear it for you next summer."

"It's the same to wear it for others," Qin said.

"The slits are way too long and I couldn't wear it for others." Despite herself, tears rolled down her cheeks. She fell into Qin

Shan's arms, saying, "I don't like others to see my legs. . ."

Qin Shan finally stopped breathing after he had struggled for two whole snowy days. People from all over Lizhen came to help Li Aijie with the funeral, but she was the only one who kept wake for the dead. Li Aijie wore that diamond blue soft silk cheongsam indoors and stayed by the stove and her husband, from morning till evening and from evening till dawn. She did not change her attire until the day the funeral procession was held.

The coffin pit was hard to dig during the cold winter season, so that small amount of frozen earth was not enough to cover the coffin. The established practice was to use a cartload of coal cinders to cover the coffin. When spring came the next year and the weather became warm, people would re-cover the grave with new earth. As the funeral manager was about to send people to fetch coal cinders, Li Aijie suddenly stopped them, saying, "Qin Shan does not like coal cinders."

The funeral manager first thought that Li Aijie was too grieved to think clearly. He was about to comfort and persuade her, when she suddenly brought out some large gunnysacks from the warehouse and walked to the entrance of the vegetable cellar. She opened the door and said to some strong young men, "Fill the bags with potatoes."

Everybody understood what Li Aijie meant and all started to fill the bags. Five bags were filled with potatoes within an hour.

People of Lizhen experienced an unusual funeral. Five large bags of potatoes stood by Qin Shan's coffin. A piece of white cloth was tied up on Li Aijie's head as a sign of mourning and she followed immediately behind the hearse all the way to the graveyard despite funeral manager's dissuasion. Qin Shan's cof-

fin was lowered into the pit and when people had scattered the
thin frozen earth on the coffin, it was still only sparsely covered
and some parts of the red cover were visible. Li Aijie stepped
forward and began to empty the bags of potatoes on the coffin.
The potatoes span and rolled violently on the coffin, but finally
united and gathered together to make Qin Shan's grave round
and complete. The sunshine, looking tired after the snow, penetrated the spaces between the potatoes, filling the grave with the
warm flavour of a good harvest. Looking at the grave with relief, Li Aijie thought that when the Milky Way was clear and
bright, Qin Shan would recognise his potato field at one glance.
And he would smell that special fragrance of the potato flowers.

Li Aijie was the last person to leave Qin Shan's grave. She had
not gone but two or three steps, when she heard a rustling noise
behind her. A round and plump potato rolled down the top of
the grave and stopped right in front of her, like a pampered
child asking for a mother's love. Li Aijie looked at that potato
with love and affection. In a soft voice she demanded, "Are you
still following me?"

February 25, 1995
Translated by Li Ziliang

Lost in the Ox Pen

BAOZHUI was listening to the oxen chewing their cud in the dark night. The sound produced by the mixing of fodder and saliva plunged him into customary reminiscing. He felt as if something important was wrapped in the sound, but the abysmal memories were impenetrable. He had to give up.

Maybe it was because Stepfather was about to die that he had come to the pen to talk to Baozhui almost every day. Sometimes he would feel Baozhui's head without speaking a word, as turbid tears spilled from his eyes. "Are you hungry, uncle?" Baozhui asked, for he himself would cry whenever he was hungry.

Stepfather tossed his head, his greenish-yellow face twitching. "You go sleep in the bedroom when I'm dead," he said, taking Baozhui by the hand, trembling.

"I like to stay with the oxen," Baozhui said, smiling. "Hua'er will have a baby soon."

Hua'er was a brown and white cow whose left cheek had on it a white spot in the shape of an orchid, something that made her look prettier than Flatface and Di'er. Di'er was a three year old black ox, the main plow puller. Flatface was an aged, short, dark-brown bull. Its thick tail easily got smeared with Flatface's dung. Baozhui would express his annoyance by thumping its belly in the evening, while he filled its trough. "Don't be so greedy! Take your meals regularly," he commanded.

That was what Mother had often preached to him. Now he was telling Flatface the same. Flatface would care nothing about it all. It never in the least reined in its appalling appetite, leading his personal hygiene from bad to worse. Baozhui had tried to tie up its tail with a rope and hang it high up on the railing. However, hardly had he tied the rope to its tail when Flatface deposited a pile of dung, which it forthwith rolled up and flung in his face. He was so infuriated that he felt like cutting that tail off.

"I'll cut off your tail to feed the wolf!" Baozhui threatened, untying the rope from the tail.

Stepfather had not come to the pen for several days in a row. Every time Xue'er came to serve him his meals Baozhui would ask, "Is my uncle dead yet?"

"You're the one who is dying!" Xue'er would clench her teeth and retort vindictively.

Xue'er was Baozhui's half-sister. Skinny and with a dislike for fatty food, she had large, black eyes that revealed waywardness. Mother said Xue'er had round worms in her belly.

The sound of cud chewing faded. With a smack of his lips Baozhui closed his eyes. Soon after he fell asleep a strong shaft of light stabbed his eyes and a repulsive smell of sour sweat attacked him. "Wake up, Baozhui! Get up and go to your uncle. He's dying, and he wishes to see you," Mother cried in a hoarse voice.

"Don't let it hurt my eyes," Baozhui groaned, pointing at the flashlight.

Mother quickly shifted the light and focused it on the rail, where the oxen were tethered, the three knots in the shape of plum blossoms looking sedate and beautiful.

Baozhui sat up.

"Go quickly. Your uncle can't wait for you much longer," Mother urged him. "Though he's only your stepfather he's been good to you. When you decided to stay in the pen he made it warmer than an actual bedroom. And he sent meals to you every day. Baozhui. . ."

"I'm not going back to any bedroom," Baozhui said, lying back. "I'll sleep with the oxen."

"Please go!" Mother entreated him, bending down to touch her son's forehead. "I'll make fried pancake with onion for you!"

"With potato slivers rolled in?" Baozhui's stomach jumped with excitement.

Mother nodded.

Baozhui sat up again. He deemed Mother's face to be as ugly as a frozen cabbage and her hair as dirty as Flatface's tail. He put on his shoes and left the pen for a nice breakfast at dawn. It was a little cold outside. The stars leaped like crickets in the courtyard and he saw the lamplight in the house. He became frightened the moment he opened the door. He winced and trembled. The atmosphere in the room drove him to the brink of tears. "I want to go back to the pen," he said mournfully.

"Baozhui. . ." Mother said. "Do you want me to kneel down before you?"

"Bao. . .zhui. . ." Stepfather's voice floated over like a small boat tossed on the sea.

Mother pushed Baozhui into the room and closed the door behind her.

Baozhui couldn't stop shivering. He saw Xue'er feeding Stepfather water from a yellow mug. Stepfather was leaning on the *kang*, eyes wide open, arms stiff as dry wood blocks.

Mother ushered Baozhui to the *kang*. Xue'er stared at him, poured the rest of the water in the mug down on the floor and walked toward the window.

Stepfather's lips squirmed like earthworms. He said breathlessly, "I'm dying. Promise you'll come and live in here. You'll live separately from mummy and Xue'er."

"Mummy will live with you," Baozhui said.

"But I'm dying. She can't live with me any more." Stepfather said.

"There will be another uncle to live with her," Baozhui said.

"You—bastard—" Mother shouted at the top of her voice and dealt him a heavy blow.

Baozhui staggered, steadied himself and looked at Stepfather nonplused.

"I want to live with the oxen," Baozhui said. "Hua'er is having a baby."

Stepfather looked at Baozhui affectionately, as large tears flowed down his sunken cheeks.

"Uncle—" Baozhui suddenly said. "Won't you come back when you're dead?"

Stepfather said "hum—", as tears continued to flow.

"Then I have a question to ask," Baozhui said. "Why do oxen chew the cud?"

Stepfather used to be a vet. He knew all about livestock.

"Their stomachs are divided into four compartments," Stepfather said. "When grass is swallowed it first passes into the rumen, then to the reticulum, whence it returns to the mouth to be masticated, and then, then—"

"Then it's swallowed again?" Baozhui asked, his eyes riveted on Stepfather.

Stepfather nodded wearily and said, "The swallowed pulp finally goes into the psalterium and the abomasum for digestion."

Baozhui misheard "digesting compartment" for "disgusting compartment". He couldn't help laughing. "Stupid oxen! Why would they move the fragrant grass into the disgusting compartment? Is that where the grass turns into dung?"

Stepfather's tears flowed faster. He tried in vain to give Baozhui's hand a pull, but each struggle dragged him farther away from his stepson.

Baozhui was thinking that he had to give the oxen more fodder, so he turned to go.

Mother stopped Baozhui, saying in a choking voice, "Won't you thank your uncle for bringing you up?"

"He's dying," said Baozhui. "Even if I thanked him, he wouldn't remember it for long. It would hurt his brain too."

"You stupid!" Mother yelled.

Baozhui turned from Mother and went out. Xue'er was seated on the threshold, weeping. Baozhui strode across to her and said, "You are not dying. Why are you crying?"

"I won't give you a darned thing to eat tomorrow," Xue'er said between her teeth, her finger pointed at Baozhui's back.

"Fried green onion pancake, rolled with potato slivers," Baozhui said gleefully.

"You're daydreaming!" Xue'er spat out.

No sooner had Baozhui entered the pen than Hua'er lowed at him. Her little master had never gone out during the night before. She must have been worried about him. Di'er mooed gently too. Even the hottempered Flatface echoed a greeting. Baozhui was moved, and hurried to fetch them more fodder. On the way to the haystack he stumbled over the hay chopper. He got up and chided it: "You'll have to work tomorrow. Why did you trip me up instead of going to sleep?"

The hay undulated softly in the trough. "Were you worried? My uncle is dying. He wanted to see me," Baozhui said to his companions. "Now I know your stomachs have four compartments. The last one is disgusting," he said, feeling Hua'er's round belly.

Hua'er, Di'er and Flatface started chewing the cud after swallowing the hay. Baozhui fell asleep on the *kang*.

The fog made the morning at the pen look very unreal. On foggy days Baozhui would feel a greater urge to cry. Sitting on the *kang* and looking around at the misty pen, he couldn't figure out why the fog came every year.

The pen railing lying across the trough was supported by two sturdy columns. The rails were made of birch wood; the dark spots on them resembled the eyes, big and small, of a crowd— with some shining bright, others dull and stupid. The three plum blossom knots trembled in the fog, like real flowers in full bloom. Baozhui had to come into contact with the trough twice a day: In the morning he untied the three plum blossom knots to let the oxen free. In the evening he tied them up again. Every time he tied or untied them his heart beat fast, as if something important was happening in that instant. And yet, however hard he tried to recall, he could not remember anything, just as he had tried in vain to recall anything when hearing the oxen chew the cud.

Baozhui was gazing at the pen railing in the fog when the door opened. A bright ray of light shot in like a geyser, and the fog drifted in too. Then he heard Xue'er's crisp voice:

"Your breakfast, Baozhui."

As Stepfather's illness worsened she was the one who served Baozhui his meals.

Baozhui gave no reply.

Xue'er quickly walked to a dinner table by the south wall and put a bowl and a plate on it. She was wearing a bright green shirt. The three oxen lowed at the sight of fresh green in the dim light.

"Fried pancakes with potato slivers rolled in!" Xue'er said. "Don't eat them all at once! Leave two for lunch!"

Baozhui gave no answer.

"Mum says it's foggy and the road is slippery so you shouldn't take Hua'er out today. If she fell the baby in her belly would die," Xue'er said glibly.

Baozhui said yes and then asked, "Is uncle dead?"

"You're dead!" Xue'er dashed over and posed herself before Baozhui. "How would you get fried pancakes to eat if he died? You silly!"

"How can you stay so harsh when you have worms in your stomach?" Baozhui said.

"Only a dog will have worms in its stomach!" Xue'er leapt up, looking like a green parrot.

"Why is uncle not yet dead?" Baozhui said despondently.

Xue'er left the pen in a fit of anger. She turned at the door and said, "Don't take Hua'er out. It's foggy and the road is slippery."

Baozhui jumped down from the *kang* for a bite of the pancake. He laid it flat on the table and rolled the potato slivers in. Strangely the delicacy at the cost of seeing uncle on his sick bed had not brought him much happiness. His stomach seemed filled with cotton. Any special delicacy would seem out of place. He left the table after swallowing just one bite.

From the low eastern window one could see that the mist out there was still quite heavy.

Baozhui jumped onto the trough and steadied himself so that his head showed above the railing. The three plum blossom knots were gazing at him emotionally. Baozhui untied two. Di'er and Flatface ambled toward the door. When Hua'er's turn came he hesitated. He jumped down from the trough and said to Hua'er while touching her nose, "Walk slowly today. If you fall the baby in your belly will feel the pain too."

Hua'er gave two gentle moos in consent.

Baozhui rolled up the two pancakes and put them in his lunch bag. Then he took up the water jar and went out of the pen with the oxen.

The mist was flowing fast over the land. The sun was moving like a hedgehog behind the thick mist. Baozhui's eyes were blurred. The road under his feet seemed painted with lard. He shook unsteadily as he stepped on it. Flatface showed the style of the elder, marching ahead; Di'er followed close behind, while Hua'er kept by Baozhui's side obediently. The four passed a number of houses through the heavy mist. The dark fences looked like herrings swimming on water. The lonesome barks of a dog was followed by the golden crow of a rooster. Baozhui and Hua'er stopped simultaneously, waiting for the crows to die down. They all liked the sound. Sometimes a few passers-by went by brushing across Baozhui's shoulder. Though the faces were hard to recognize the voice was familiar.

"Grazing the oxen?" Old Zhang droned. He liked drinking. That's why his tongue sounded disobedient.

"Hua'er hasn't delivered her baby yet?" asked Aunt Xing the beancurd maker. She spoke fast, and her mouth always breathed onion.

"Can your uncle still stand it?" The questioner was none other than Lame Li with his three years old son Redwood in his grab. He kept that mournful look ever since his wife had died. He loitered along the small paths of the village every day. He was ready to join in for dinner with whoever invited him. His wife had been dead for a year. He and his son had dined by turns in every house of the village. He would ask Baozhui about his uncle every time they met.

Baozhui's answers were all brief:

"Yeah."

"Not yet."

"Dying."

Baozhui and the three oxen went to a grazing field one kilometre away, with a thicker mist and more tender grass. Baozhui could soon hear the oxen grazing with their head bent close to the ground, producing pleasant sounds reminiscent of the softness and purity of the grass. Standing in a grove of grass he tried to catch a handful of fog. Failing that, he tried again. Nothing! His hand remained empty. He couldn't understand how he could fail to catch something right in his visual scope.

Baozhui's stepfather thought he would leave the world that night. But after midnight his breath returned to normal. To prove himself still alive he coughed. The woman beside him turned and asked listlessly, "You alright?"

He said "yeah" and attempted to walk. To his surprise he managed to walk to the eastern window. The sky was hazy, the white fog surging, creating a heavenly atmosphere as described in legends. His heart smarted again, tears streaking down silently. Seeing that he was now okay, the woman dressed herself and arose to cook. She said as she stoked the fire, "Yesterday evening I promised Baozhui I'd make a fried pancake for him. He wants potato slivers too. He's not silly at all when it comes to eating."

Xue'er soon got up too. As soon as she came out of her bedroom she shouted to Mother in the kitchen, "There's a heavy fog outside. You can't see anything. Everything is confused."

"It's the fog month," the woman said matter-of-factly, heaving a sad sigh.

"What's the fog made of?" Xue'er asked herself melancholically.

"Tell your brother not to take Hua'er out today when you serve him breakfast. In the thick mist Hua'er might fall and hurt the baby in her belly."

Xue'er cried out at the sight of the dough Mother was kneading, "Are you really going to make pancaeke for Baozhui?"

"Xue'er!" Baozhui's stepfather turned from the eastern window and said, "Don't call him Baozhui all the time! Call him Elder Brother—"

"Need I call a fool brother?" Xue'er said scornfully. "He stays with the oxen every day. No wonder they say we're keeping four oxen!"

"Three oxen," the woman corrected, "the fourth one isn't

born yet."

"Baozhui is an ox too!" Xue'er said and ran to the courtyard
to feed the chicks.

The fog did not thin out until around ten o'clock in the morning. The sun was still misty, like an oil lamp behind a paper
pasted window. Baozhui's stepfather drank some soup and went
towards the pen on the other side of the courtyard. The woman
followed meticulously. He pushed the door open, looked at the
kang and fireplace he had personally made as well as the familiar objects hung on the wall: roe deer skin, horse mane, rolls of
coir ropes, a rat catcher and a fishing net etc... Tears rolled
down again as he remembered what a smart boy Baozhui was
when he first met him.

"Why is Hua'er absent—" the woman suddenly said in agita-
tion. "What a fool! I told him not to take her out in the fog.
She's having a baby. What if she fell and the baby aborted?"

The woman quickly turned back to the house in search of
Xue'er, "Why didn't you send my message to Baozhui? Hua'er is
not in the pen!"

"I told him—" Xue'er argued loudly. "I told him twice!"

"Where could he lead them to today?"

"How could I know?" Xue'er said. "We won't know till he's
back in the evening."

"He will be back in the evening. Will Hua'er be back too?"
The woman cursed the fog month till her lips twitched and her
breath ran out. She then set her mind to look for Baozhui. She
had just changed into rubber shoes. Suddenly remembering that
her husband had been mortally sick in bed for half a month but
was miraculously able to walk she felt ill at ease. She feared mis-

fortune would befall him the moment she went out. Though as far as her future was concerned the oxen were more important than her husband, she still chose her husband.

Baozhui's stepfather turned his eyes to the white birch railing. The Baozhui of eight years ago again returned in his mind's eye. He had liked him at first sight. He had a strong build and he liked laughing. His own father had died of snake bite while cutting grass. At that time Baozhui's mother was not so dirty. The bedding on the *kang* was well washed and smelt soap. The kitchen utensils shined with cleanliness. He had married her happily though he was two years younger than her. At that time they had had only one room and the whole family shared one *kang*, with Baozhui on the edge. During their honeymoon the man would sleep with the woman almost every night. On moonlit nights he could see Baozhui's face when he was sound asleep. Every time Baozhui turned or sleep talked he would shiver as if the deceased man's soul was watching him from a corner. He had sworn that he would build a house soon so that seven year old Baozhui could have a room of his own. But the fog month came before his house was built.

The village they lived in was surrounded by a hill on three sides and faced with water. Every June the fog drifted endlessly. The fog would not thin out except at noon. For lack of sunlight the crops grew very slow during this month. The fog was said to last no more than three or four days, but here it could last a month. Even meteorologists on field survey here could not find a reasonable explanation. In the end popular legend held sway. Legend said that three hundred years ago a vagrant fairy god passed here and saw well growing crops, herds of oxen and am-ple storage of food. Everything looked fine, except that many men were scolding their wives for their ugliness. Puzzled, he consulted the humiliated, weeping women and found that it was in June, when the sun was bright and farm work was idle that the women were complained of most. The fairy god smiled and turned June into a fog month, suffocating the pungent sun. The women in the surging fog looked like fairies. The men became gentler and happier, as if their faded tender feelings had revived in the humidity.

Baozhui's stepfather had wanted his wife more than ever during that fog month. One evening they were having a great time in the thick encirclement of the fog when Baozhui woke up without their knowing it, sat up watching their undulating shadows and finally laughed. That laugh devastated stepfather's passion. Extremely ashamed, he moved tremulously and timidly away from the woman.

The following morning he followed Baozhui into the pen besieged in the fog. He asked Baozhui meticulously, "What did you see last night?"

"I saw you and mum folded in a mass," Baozhui said conscientiously.

Baozhui leapt to the trough, untied the rope on the railing and suddenly asked, "Uncle, why did you make the same noise as the oxen chewing the cud?"

This was the moment when he had leapt onto the trough and punched Baozhui down on the railing where his head landed heavily and with an "Ah" he dropped like a current of water down into the trough. At first he thought Baozhui had merely fainted. So he took him back to the house and said to the woman busy in the kitchen, "Baozhui knocked his head on the railing."

"He's a nimble boy. How could he have his own head knocked?" The woman cried and ran to test Baozhui's breath. She felt it and said light-heartedly, "He's fainted. He'll be alright after a good sleep."

Baozhui slept in the fog for the entire day. When he got up it was another foggy morning. He saw everything strange. His eyes were dull. He did not know when his mother called him.

"Does your head ache?" Stepfather asked.

"No," Baozhui said, looking at the fog outside.

In the evening Baozhui demanded to live in the pen. He said he could not live with people. Stepfather thought he was just confused for one or two days, so he did not put it in heart. He went to the pen and erected a bed for him therein. Thus started Baozhui's life with the oxen. He refused to go back to a human house. Later they found Baozhui speaking illogically without stop. Being gluttonous and fond of sleep, he looked tearful on foggy days. They then discovered that Baozhui had lost part of his consciousness and had become mentally retarded. For several times the woman cried into convulsions. She then was pregnant and the baby in her womb got affected. As a result, Xue'er was born premature. Stepfather was all regret. He could not figure out why one punch should have ruined his stepson's future. In his eyes the white birch rail was no different from a slaughtering knife. Not daring to tell his wife the truth, he refurbished the pen and built a *kang* therein. He took the trouble of serving his meals and talked to him in the hope of opening up his gate of memory. In the depth of winter, when the north wind was roaring he would get up every midnight and add firewood to Baozhui's *kang* and feed the oxen. Baozhui could not go to school like other children. He had to herd the oxen every day.

He liked the oxen. He gave each of the three a name. On the morning of every Lunar New Year's Day stepfather would come to the pen to put new clothes on him, paste the papercut Chinese character "Happiness" on the window and give him a hand-made lantern. Baozhui's favourite was golden pumpkin lanterns. He made him one of these every year. At midnight when everyone else was either eating dumplings or letting out firecrackers he would bring Baozhui out to the courtyard to let him see and hear the fireworks. The overjoyed Baozhui would eat two plates of dumplings at a stretch.

The birth of Xue'er did not bring him any happiness—he felt that it was somehow connected with Baozhui's illness. He had lost his sexual ability when Xue'er was two years old. He never thought of doing that soul-stirring thing again. A sense of guilt made him reticent. His health was very much taxed by all this, and all the special prescriptions his wife had sought out for him had proved ineffective. She became more and more bad-tempered, her face looked swollen, and she never bothered to dress up again. By the time her husband was reduced to a bag of bones she offered to borrow money so that he could get treatment in the city. He flatly refused, claiming that they must save all the money for treating Baozhui's head. The woman then wept and praised him for being so kind to his stepson. Baozhui must have done a lot of good in his previous life, she said.

The fog made the white birch railing look thicker. Fixing his eyes on that sinister railing, Stepfather felt like munching it up like a crisp bone, swallowing it or dumping it into hell. Four years previously he had spent all his earnings to build another house. As a result, Xue'er had a small *kang* of her own. He knew he was about to leave this world, and he wanted Baozhui to return to the house. That way he might change for the better. However, what Baozhui had said the night before made it impossible for him to breath his last in peace. He had said that when Stepfather died there would come another uncle—so Baozhui would still have no space of his own. He blamed himself for his negligence.

And now he could not build any more rooms.

"Baozhui—" he called in a weak voice in the direction of the pale white railing.

The railing occupied a prominent position in the pen. It was right over the trough in the middle of it. The white bark had been polished bright by the ropes, and the dark spots of different sizes looked as clear as eyes. Except for the pen railing lying uniquely horizontal, all the objects were vertical. The vertical columns, the walls and the door all served as a foil to the white railing, which seemed to hover in mid air. To Stepfather monsters with long, sharp gnashing teeth had existed only in legends. Now he saw a real monster—the railing!

"I must get rid of this monster," he said to himself.

Looking around the pen he espied a tool box in the northwest corner. Out of it he picked a small axe he used to cleave pine branches with. He then returned to the trough in an attempt to climb up, but the strength in him failed. He could not get into the trough however hard he tried. All he could do was look stupidly at the towering railing. He had been facing it no more than two minutes when he felt a thicker fog stalking him. The white railing hid cunningly in the fog, looking as strange as lightning behind clouds. His eyes were blurred, first by the boundless white, then by the immense black, and finally by the stimulating purple. Tottering to his feet, he shouted "Baozhui" at the railing and fell prostrate on the floor. He had the axe, rusty from long disuse, in his hand when he died.

It was supper time when Baozhui got back with the oxen. Flatface and Di'er were walking in front, he and Hua'er behind. The mist had grown even thicker by the evening. Baozhui walked very slowly. He feared Hua'er would stumble. He had decided to ask uncle one more question if he was not yet dead.

He heard the sound of sawing and polishing before he entered the family courtyard. He stopped to pat Hua'er and said, "Ah, listen! Do you hear anything?"

After a moment of silence Hua'er raised her head and gave a brief low in the affirmative.

Baozhui felt that there was a crowd of people in the courtyard. The sound of the polishing of planks resembled that of wheat harvesting. He recklessly bumped into someone who responded, "Is that Baozhui?"

Baozhui said yes and asked, "What are you doing?"

"Making a coffin," the man said, unconcerned. "Your uncle has died."

"Uncle died?" Baozhui whispered and turned to Hua'er, "But I have a question for him."

Baozhui suddenly started sobbing. The sound of sobbing rang out in the fog so loud that almost everyone heard it. "Who is crying?" they asked simultaneously.

"Baozhui."

"Baozhui's mourning the death of his uncle."

"Baozhui finds it hard to part with his uncle."

Everybody jabbered at the same time:

"He cries more sincerely than a real son would."

"That shows that he really loved his stepfather."

Baozhui's sobbing rekindled Mother's weeping and Xue'er's strident voice joined in too. People were rushing in and out, consoling the old and young by turns. Baozhui was finally led to the ox pen, with Hua'er following behind mute. Di'er and Flatface had been expecting them. A man turned on the light—a dim, yellow bulb that shone over the white railing, the chopper sticking out of it and the *kang*. Baozhui trembled, a desolate feeling rising in his heart. Seeing that he had stopped crying, the man closed the door and went back to the coffin.

Baozhui jumped up onto the trough and tied the three oxen to the railing. Uncle would show up before his eyes every time a plum blossom knot was tied. The question he wanted to ask uncle was: How could he tie plum blossom knots? That was the only question in his mind while he was alone in the meadow in the daytime. Now he would never learn the answer.

Baozhui jumped down from the trough to feed the oxen bean cakes and then sat on the *kang* gazing at the three knots on the railing. Hua'er left the trough to munch a pile of hay nearby, which made the rope on its neck tighten for a moment. "No one can unsettle the flower I make!" Baozhui suddenly blurted out.

Stepfather's red coffin was enveloped in the thick mist, which made the fiery red appear somewhat subdued. Stepfather was encoffined and buried after being displayed for three days. Early in the morning there came a wagon to carry the bier. Someone placed a mourning hat on Baozhui's head and tied a long mourning sash around his waist, which made him quite displeased. The foggy courtyard was filled with human figures. A white streamer hung from a pole at the entrance to the yard like a large reed. Mother came to the pen to give Baozhui instructions, telling him to cry aloud when seeing uncle off, to kowtow in all four directions and shout, "Go in peace, uncle!"

"Do you understand?" Mother asked in a sad and resentful voice. Her lips were full of blisters, and, probably as a result of rubbing at floods of tears and her running nose, the sleeves of her cotton-padded coat looked hard and white, as if starched.

Baozhui gave no reply.

"Your uncle was so kind to you. You should pay your respects to him. He will bless you from the nether world so that you'll recover," Mother impressed on him.

Baozhui could not understand why Mother sounded as if there was something wrong with him when in fact he felt perfectly normal.

No sooner had Mother gone than Baozhui took off the mourning hat and threw it on the pile of hay. He also took off the white cloth sash, so that the blood in his body flowed freely again. He sprang up onto the trough, untied the three plum blossom knots and then took Di'er, Flatface and Hua'er outside. As they passed through the yard many people pointed to the oxen and asked Baozhui if he was going to see his uncle off.

Baozhui said, "No, I'm going to pasture the oxen."

"What if your mother gets angry?"

"I don't care," said Baozhui. "Uncle is dead. He wouldn't know even if I did see him off."

Nobody went forward to stop him when people saw Baozhui walk on the wet village road with the oxen, nor did anyone inform Mother in the house. Baozhui was unfortunate enough. Why take the trouble to have him attend a funeral?

The fog made the day as hazy as dusk, and the dusk was darker than the dusk of the past. As Baozhui came back with the oxen he could faintly see the round paper money scattered on the way which was trodden into shreds by oxen hoofs.

Mother went forward to greet him as soon as he entered the yard. She felt Hua'er's head without a word and heaved a long breath.

"Is uncle gone?" Baozhui asked.

"Yes," Mother said peacefully. "Will you still sleep in the pen today?"

"Yes," Baozhui said. "I like to stay with the oxen."

"Didn't your uncle promise to let you live in the house when he was gone?" Mother said slowly.

"No," Baozhui said resolutely. "Hua'er is having a baby soon."

"So you'll go back to the house after Hua'er has given birth?"

"After that we'll have more oxen. They can't do without me." Baozhui went back to the pen with the oxen. He leapt onto the trough, fixed the three plum blossom knots and started drinking the oxen.

The light in the pen was dim. In the still air, the sound of drinking was very crisp. The door opened, and in came Xue'er in a blue shirt. She had a bowl in hand and a white ribbon at the end of her pigtail. She silently put the bowl on the dinner table and then fixed her eyes on Baozhui.

"Did you go and see uncle off today?" Baozhui asked.

Xue'er said "yes".

"Were there many people?" Baozhui asked again.

Xue'er again said "yes".

The oxen kept drinking.

"Elder—brother—" Xue'er suddenly said in a crying voice.

"Were you upset when I called you Baozhui?"

Baozhui tossed his head, "Baozhui's my name. Why do you call me elder brother?"

"Because you're my kinsman, and you're older than me," Xue'er replied.

"Flatface is also older than you. Do you call him elder brother too?"

"Oxen are different," Xue'er explained patiently. "Only man has brothers and sisters."

"Oh," Baozhui said melancholically. "So I'm elder brother."

The three oxen lay prostrate on the hay after drinking enough water.

"Why wasn't I called elder brother?" Baozhui asked with bewilderment.

"Because I hated you. Dad never took me in his arms when he was alive. All he cared about was you. He thought about your pen all the time. As I fed him water when he was dying he kept calling your name. And yet I'm his own daughter!"

"So you hated me?" Baozhui asked.

Xue'er nodded and said, "No more now, since he's dead."

"Why?"

"There's no longer anyone who loves you as much as dad," Xue'er said, "Why should I keep hating you?"

"So you hate my uncle?" Baozhui asked again.

Xue'er tossed her head with tears in her eyes and said, "I pity him. Mother scolded him every midnight. He would cry whenever she cursed him, and he said 'Baozhui Baozhui' when he cried."

"How do you know?" Baozhui asked.

"I heard it," Xue'er said. "Mum cursed him so loudly I could hear in my bedroom. Later I'd wake up every midnight and hear mum dressing him down. She cursed him more vehemently in the fog month."

"What did she say?"

"Good-for-nothing," Xue'er replied. "That's the only word she used."

Baozhui was bewilderment itself.

"It means useless," Xue'er explained.

"What does mum use uncle for in the middle of the night?" Baozhui asked.

"I don't know either," said Xue'er.

"Why would uncle call my name when he was scolded?" Baozhui asked again.

"I don't know either." Xue'er said. "Was it you who made him good for nothing?"

Baozhui became serious. "I can herd oxen. If I'm not a good-for-nothing, how can I make him one? Mum's full of rubbish. Uncle could do all kinds of work, he even knew an ox's stomach has four compartments. Wasn't he great? He didn't know how to tie plum blossom knots though. How could I do it when neither mum nor uncle knew how?"

"You learnt it from your own father!" Xue'er said.

"Where is he?" Baozhui asked excitedly.

"In the earth." Xue'er pouted her lips and said. "They say he died a long time ago."

Baozhui uttered an "Ah" despondently.

"Lame Li came with Redwood to our home today right after dad is buried." Xue'er said.

"Did mum feed them?" Baozhui asked.

"Yes," said Xue'er. "She gave some of your old clothes to

Redwood too."

"Aren't you happy about their coming?" Baozhui asked.

"I don't even want to speak to mum again because she gives them food right after daddy's death."

"Then don't speak to her."

"But there's only two of us in the house," Xue'er said woefully. "I'm afraid she'll be angry if I don't talk. Would she curse me at midnight when she could curse nobody else?"

"Why should she curse you?" Baozhui said earnestly. "You didn't let round worms enter her stomach."

Xue'er burst into a short laugh and looked at Baozhui tearfully.

"Don't you worry. If she scolds you at midnight you may come to the pen and see your elder bro-ther—" Baozhui stammered at the word "brother".

Xue'er said "yes" and pointed to the food, "Have some food. The heat will be gone soon. It's left over from the funeral feast."

Baozhui turned his eyes to the funeral food.

Hua'er finally delivered her baby—a black and white ox with an ear rolled up like a flower bud, which was why Baozhui named it Rollear. Rollear brought unprecedented harmony and joy to the family. Xue'er came to play with Rollear every day. She either used pink hair ribbons to wind its legs or used thin bamboo strips to prick its black nose tip. Mother too came to feed it bean grout every night. Hua'er was very affectionate to Rollear. She constantly licked its face. Di'er loved it too. Only the dirty-tailed Flatface tried to scare it with a couple of shrill cries. As Rollear did not mind it at all Flatface had to stop his pranks. A week later the glossy Rollear started loitering around. It was very naughty, by turns pushing up green seedlings with its snout or kicking wood piles down. It was only while watching the fog that it became peaceful. It looked moody whenever the white mist had mystified the people and environment it had just been acquainted with.

Baozhui's was now an expanded group as he went to the grazing field again. He thought his group would continue to grow till he was finally surrounded by oxen. He would know the temper of every ox and understand the implication of each of their acts. There will be more and more plum blossom knots blooming in a cluster on the white birch railing. How great he would look walking on the village road with a herd of oxen!

One dusk before the end of the fog month, Xue'er rushed into the pen in high spirits right after Baozhui and his oxen had returned. "Brother, mummy drove Lame Li out of the house today. He won't be coming any more." She panted out.

"I don't care," Baozhui said in a dull tone.

"You know why?" Xue'er said in a hushed voice. "Lame Li said when he became part of the family he'd send you to the gold mine to watch over the gold. He said you'd get the job because you're too silly to steal. He said if you went there you'd make money and save food for the family. And he has already come to terms with the employer."

Baozhui looked at Xue'er in great surprise.

"On hearing this mummy started cursing Lame Li—" Xue'er stretched out her breast and mimicked in a contrived loud voice, "Get lost! Don't you expect to make a fool of our Baozhui! When his uncle was alive he treated Baozhui better than his own child. Whoever dares to maltreat him will be driven off my threshold!"

"So Lame Li went?" Baozhui asked.

"Yeah." Xue'er said.

"Good!" Baozhui exclaimed.

Xue'er then said sheepishly, "Brother, you need not worry about my being scolded by mother at midnight any more because she sleeps with me in her arms every night and she helps me catch the lice in my hair."

Baozhui smiled in relief. He leapt to the trough and went to the railing to have the oxen tied up. He was tying the plum blossom knots very deftly when Xue'er said to him:

"Brother, I dreamt of dad and you last night."

Baozhui jumped down and looked at Xue'er inquisitively.

"I dreamt of dad celebrating the New Year with you," Xue'er said in a quivering voice. "It was dark, and snowing. Dad was letting out firecrackers with you in the yard. The firecrackers were very loud. Dad was trying to cover your ears lest you panicked."

Baozhui was on the verge of tears. The dream, like the fog, was not to be caught. He did not know how it felt to be dreaming.

"I dreamt of him looking at Rollear in the pen too. He reached out his hand to touch its nose. Rollear kicked at him because it didn't know him."

"How could Rollear do that?" Baozhui said sentimentally. "It was uncle!"

Listening to the oxen's sound of chewing the cud, Baozhui once again tried his best to recall what important event was enveloped in the sound. He strained his brain till it numbed, but memories remained fenced in insurmountable high walls. He turned on the light to look at that white birch railing again. The pitch dark spots, like tireless eyes, were gazing at the plum blossom knots. His memories were flimsy like the white mist and as dark as infinite night. Baozhui stayed in a trance for some time before looking at the cute, slumbering Rollear. "I'm happy with the oxen. Why should I recall the unrecoverable past?" he said to himself.

Baozhui turned off the light and went to bed. His sleep was devoid of dream and thus clean and transparent. In the morning he was suddenly woken up by a creak of the door and a shaft of light. He sat up and saw that Rollear had pushed the door ajar. Hua'er, Di'er and Flatface all looked emotionally at the long awaited sun outside.

The fog month passed.

Baozhui got off and walked to the entrance of the pen.

Tilting its head on one side, Rollear looked at the swirling sun with much surprise. Baozhui slapped on its buttocks and said, "The sun is shining. Go out and enjoy yourself."

Rollear tried to move its hoofs but winced back abruptly. Baozhui remembered Rollear was born in the fog month and had never seen the sun. It was scared by the dazzling brightness. Baozhui strode across the threshold and demonstrated by walking steadily in the yard and beckoning it. Rollear responded tenderly and then followed him timidly out to the yard.

With its back bent, Rollear would lower its head every step it moved, as if it wanted to see if it had trampled the sunlight to pieces and made it obscure.

Translated by Wang Chiying

Silver Plates

HU Sheng's recent coldness prodded Ji Ai's desire to find a job in the city. In the past, Hu Sheng would always come to see Ji Ai right after his return. He would give her small presents such as a frilled cloth bag, red plexiglass hairpins or ornamented black gauze gloves. He actually bought her whatever urban women found fashionable. Ji Ai had very round corner lips. When she smiled she had the habit of pursing up her lips without baring her teeth. The smile in the corner of her lips shone like the hot summer sun. Bathed in it, a man would automatically say something sweet. Every time she got something from Hu Sheng she claimed it useless—a sheer waste of money. But her lip corners would turn rounder, showing the smiles crowded therein.

Hu Sheng had been a construction worker in town for three years. He came home twice a year—for the autumn harvest and the Spring Festival. Summer was the most lonesome season for Ji Ai. Busy and sweating all the time, she found her days as pale and lifeless as the winter snow. She couldn't help missing Hu Sheng. Every time she went to the wheat fields she hoped the wheat would grow fast, their ears becoming heavier and heavier 'cause Hu Sheng would then be back.

As a bricklayer Hu Sheng earned a monthly income of seven hundred yuan. In fact he was the family's bread winner, paying for the fertilizer in the field and the new tiles on the roof. Better fertilization yielded better crops. His family produced the best wheat in the village. And the newly tiled roof never again leaked a drop. The girls in the village all envied him and wished to be carried over his threshold so that, red scarf off, their happy married life might begin.

However, the girls later found out that every time Hu Sheng came back he would look for Ji Ai first. Despondent, they self-consciously held her at a distance. If Ji Ai consulted them about a knitting problem, they would deliberately give her wrong instructions so that her sweater for Hu Sheng would turn out poorly. But the never-minding Ji Ai smiled as usual.

Ji Ai put under her pillow all the trinkets that Hu Sheng gave her. In her weariness they served as an effective lift to her spirits. And if she had trouble falling asleep at night she simply sat up and examined her fancy cloth bag, her gloves and hairpins one by one till her eyes blurred and these objects were transformed into Hu Sheng's tender, loving eyes. She would then hate the wheat in the fields for growing too slowly.

Hu Sheng had two married sisters and one ghostly thin elder brother. He looked crest-fallen and listless. After three years' marriage, he was still childless. It was hard to decide whose fault it was since his wife, Wu Aicui, was equally wan, sallow and sapless, looking as if she had never had a decent meal. Their parents were worried about this and pinned their hopes on their younger son's early return and early marriage to Ji Ai. The medium-sized Ji Ai was round all over—face, limbs, buttocks, earlobes and lip corners that gave her a pleasing charm. She was good at all kinds of farm work: raising pigs, cooking, harvesting and what not. Hu Sheng's parents were expecting this buxom girl to bear them some fat grandchildren once she became their daughter-in-law. And that explains the frequent exchange of visits between the two families on holiday occasions. Hu Sheng's father called his counterpart *qingjia* (parents of one's daughter-in-law or son-in-law) whenever they met.

During the first two years that he worked in town Hu Sheng bought Ji Ai fashionable things to wear, while he himself remained countrified, looking no different than before in his cloth shirt and trousers. This made her happy. She felt as though her future life with him was guaranteed.

However, Hu Sheng was actually quite cold toward her this time. He came back at an unexpected moment: neither harvest time nor Spring Festival, but green May. She was feeding the chickens in the courtyard when her brother, Ji Qing, came in with a bag of fertilizer on his shoulder and announced the news.

At first she couldn't believe it. She thought her brother was just making fun of her, so she kept on feeding the chickens.

"He had on a necktie and a pair of leather shoes, and his hair well-combed. I couldn't even recognize him," Ji Qing gasped, as he put down the fertilizer.

Ji Ai stopped her work and said in a weak voice, "Why at this hour? What's happened?"

"Nothing to fuss about," Ji Qing replied. "Maybe he's made enough money to show off now."

"He's not that kind of person," Ji Ai protested.

Though full of doubts about Hu Sheng's sudden return, Ji Ai happily went indoors to dress up. In the past Hu Sheng would

have wolfed down some food and come directly to see her. She
had always paid special attention to her attire during the harvesting season and the Spring Festival. She was wont to iron the
collar and sleeve cuffs of her shirt and apply cream to her face
until it seethed with fragrance—in the hope that the home-com-
ing Hu Sheng would be attracted to her all the more. However,
there had been times when such careful preparations fell entirely
flat. For example, the year before last, ever since the twenty-
third of December of the Chinese lunar calendar, the day when
the Kitchen God ascended into heaven, she began to dress up so
neatly every day that she felt awkward as she worked.

Ji Ai had been expecting Hu Sheng to arrive one of those
days. On the noon of the twenty-sixth, the sow that the family
raised suddenly gave birth to a litter of pigs. Ji Ai had to change
into dirty clothes and go to the pigsty to help. She sweated a lot
and her hands were stained with filthy blood as she delivered the
twelve piglets one by one. Hu Sheng came at that instant. He
laughed at the sight of her. "Twelve piglets," Ji Ai exclaimed.

"Look at the blood on your hands," Hu Sheng said.

Ji Ai felt sorry for herself. She blamed God for letting Hu
Sheng come at such an inopportune time. But Hu Sheng liked
the way she worked. All her vim and vigor were infused in her
job.

Ji Ai dressed herself in a red-flowered shirt on a green base
and a pair of black tights. She combed her hair again and again
and tied her braids with red plexiglass ribbons. After that she
fetched a basin of water, rinsed her face and pasted on a layer
of cream. She preened her eyebrows with her fingernails as she
looked herself in the mirror. Her eyes and nose were impecca-
ble, though her lips did not look red enough. She bit them with

her teeth till they turned as red as the crest of a rooster.

Ji Ai poured the water onto the ground in the courtyard. It splashed on the chickens who responded by annoyed cackling and leaps. She chuckled with amusement. By now her parents had returned from the fields. The way she dressed herself made them wonder if she was going to a fair in town.

The fair, not more than twenty kilometers away from her village, was open on the first and fifteenth of every Chinese lunar month. There she could see the frills, crochets, papercuts and headdresses that she liked. Prior to the Spring Festival, she would go with her friends to buy firecrackers, New Year couplets, chopsticks, plates, lanterns, fancy clothes, etc. If they went to the fair in summer they would try to get to the county seat early in the morning. Not wanting to have her shoes worn out on the mountain paths, she would go barefoot with her shoes in hand. Her shoes cost money while her feet did not. Even if her soles developed blisters they would heal after she pricked them with a needle and then soaked her feet in brine.

"Today is neither the first nor fifteenth day," her parents said. "Why should I go to the fair?" Ji Ai responded. "Why are you always so muddle-headed?"

The days in her parent's eyes were always the same. The only difference was that they ate pyramid-shaped rice dumplings during the Dragon-boat Festival, with moxa and calabash inserted in the door lintel, mooncakes during the Mid-Autumn Festival, dumplings on New Year's Eve, sweet rice dumplings for the Lantern Festival and pork's head on the 2nd of the lunar month of February.

"Hu Sheng's back," Ji Qing cut in, "wearing a necktie and a pair of leather shoes, his hair combed to a shine."

"Why has he come back at this time of the year?"

"Maybe he wants to build a house and marry Ji Ai," Ji Qing said.

"Who says I'm going to marry him?" Ji Ai chided him, a smile rising to her lip corners.

Knowing that Ji Ai was expecting Hu Sheng, the parents had to cook lunch. Afraid that he might dash over after a morsel of food, Ji Ai's mother took some bacon out of a jar that she prepared for cooking, and bid her daughter fetch some duck eggs as well.

"The duck eggs have been preserved for only two weeks," Ji Ai's father said. "The salt has not soaked through them."

"But Mum is concerned about her son-in-law," Ji Qing said enviously.

"Wouldn't you be treated likewise if you went to Xiuhua's?" Ji Ai retorted. "Wouldn't your mother-in-law buy meat and make dumplings for you too?"

Xiuhua had been Ji Qing's fiancee for three years. They planned to be married after this year's harvest.

Ji Qing laughed and told Ji Ai to bring the duck eggs.

Regrettably, Hu Sheng did not show up even when the sun was already high in the sky. Though short of breath because of hunger, the family waited persistently. Ji Ai became restless by about one o'clock in the afternoon. "Are you sure it was Hu Sheng?" she asked her brother.

"Yes, of course! We even greeted each other," Ji Qing said. "Come on! Let's eat."

"Yes, let's," Ji Ai's father echoed.

The family began eating around the lunch table in the courtyard. A breath of wind pushed up Ji Ai's fringed hair. She ate absent-mindedly while her elder brother ate voraciously. In the afternoon he was supposed to help fertilize Xiuhua's fields.

After lunch, the whole family went to work in the fields. Ji Ai cleared the table and did the washing up and then rinsed her greasy hands with a soap again and again until she could smell the sweet scent. Then, looking at herself in the mirror, she thought of the way Hu Sheng's furry mustache rustled against her cheeks and the tender feeling that rose in her every time he kissed her. She went to the door to watch for him in spite of herself. She could see nothing but basking pigs, leisurely wadding ducks and naked children playing. Ji Ai watched for awhile and then went back indoors to wait. Though she usually paid little attention to the clock on the wall, this afternoon she heard every tick it produced. The striking of the pendulum was even more vexing to her. Never in the past had Hu Sheng tarried so long before coming to see her when he returned. Ji Ai's soul was departing from her. When she ran to the door once again, she found the children gone but the pigs still there, their bellies upturned, and the ducks waddling across the yard. Ji Ai was disappointment itself. She felt like going to see him, but he was probably already on the way. So she went back inside, expecting him to arrive soon. A rendezvous without any interference naturally bespoke of an indescribable closeness and convenience. Yet she could hear no footsteps from outside the courtyard. All she heard was the ticking of the clock.

Ji Ai watched and watched, not realizing that the sun had already gone west. The pot-bellied pigs were whining at home and the ducks had vanished. The people working in the fields were returning home, and there was no sign of Hu Sheng.

The sad Ji Ai made supper when her parents arrived. "Have

you quarreled with Hu Sheng?" they asked in concern.

"No," she answered.

"Then why do you look so unhappy?" her father asked.

"He didn't even come," Ji Ai replied.

"Maybe he'll come in the evening," her mother tried to comfort her.

Ji Ai ate supper absent-mindedly. Her parents did not have much of an appetite either. Ji Qing had gone to Xiuhua's where he'd have supper and remain until late at night before coming home whistling.

She did the washing up, fed the pigs, cooped the chickens, extinguished the fire in the kitchen and fetched a basin of water in which she repeatedly washed her greasy hands with soap until they gave off a fragrance. Her mother was mending some underwear while her father sat on a low bench smoking. The clock was still ticking away, as if it would never wear out. The moody Ji Ai came to the moonlit courtyard, where she was reminded of happy times spent in the past with Hu Sheng. She kept standing there and she saw no sign of Hu Sheng even when her elder brother came back whistling.

"Won't you see him at his house?" her mother whispered.

"Don't spoil him," her father commanded. "No hurry to see him. She doesn't lack pursuers."

Ji Qing went to sleep after a few words of bantering. The rest of the family went to bed too. Ji Ai turned off the light and fumbled with the things Hu Sheng had given her. She did not understand it at all. For the first time she knew what insomnia was.

Early the next morning, Ji Ai's mother went to see Hu Sheng on the pretext of asking for a shoe sample from his mother. He was sleeping. "He said he'd go and see Ji Ai today," his mother apologized. "He was too tired yesterday."

"Hu Sheng will be coming to see you soon." Ji Ai's mother came back and said. "He was too tired yesterday."

"You're real cheap!" Her father mumbled.

The family went to the fields after eating breakfast, leaving Ji Ai alone at home. She put on the same shirt and tights, and plaited her well-combed hair into a braids tied with the red plexiglass ribbon. In the morning Hu Sheng came as expected. In leather shoes and a necktie, he looked thinner and was embarrassed at the sight of her.

"Why back at this time of the year?" Ji Ai asked. "Aren't you going to work in town any more?"

"Yes I am," Hu Sheng answered. "I'll be finished if I come back to farming."

"So you plan to stay there forever?"

Hu Sheng smiled wryly.

"But you're a rural resident," Ji Ai said.

"That's not a problem," Hu Sheng replied. "Many rural residents are living a better life than the local townspeople up there."

"Townspeople are not necessarily better off, they spend a one-cent coin in eight portions," Ji Ai cackled. "Last time I went to the fair a well-dressed girl bargained endlessly for a dozen cents or so over a ceramic cup. Isn't that stinginess?"

"That's in the county seat," Hu Sheng said, tossing his head. "It's a different story in the provincial capital."

"I've never been to the provincial capital," Ji Ai said.

Hu Sheng fell silent. Ji Ai thought he'd come over to kiss her as he had in the past. So she lowered her head, her cheeks turning hot. But he only stammered, "I'm—home—to register—for marriage."

Ji Ai lifted her eyes to him in disbelief. But his expression soon revealed the truth of it. Besides, he neither kissed her nor gave her any present.

"Does she live in the city?" Ji Ai asked breathlessly.

"The contractor's niece with an amputated leg," Hu Sheng replied, nodding.

Why would he marry a disabled woman in the city when he could marry a nice girl like me? Ji Ai wondered. What a fool I was to love such an idiot!

"Beat me, Ji Ai!" Hu Sheng said. "That'll make me feel better."

Why should I beat a fool? Ji Ai thought. And she said, "Go! Don't ever come back again!"

Hu Sheng went away haltingly. He cried as he reached the entrance. He cried more bitterly as he remembered Ji Ai's round arms, legs, face, buttocks and lip corners. After staying some time indoors, Ji Ai took out all the gifts Hu Sheng had given her from under the pillow and rolled them into a bundle. She wanted to burn them in the stove, but she changed her mind as she neared the kitchen. She would do well if she put them out of sight. So she distributed them among her friends Qiuyue, Shuimei and Yanli, who were naturally pleased to have them.

After that Ji Ai went back home to make lunch. She shed tears as she gazed at the soft fire in the kitchen stove. Her sleeves were wet with tears. This was the first and only time she had ever cried for Hu Sheng. Hardly a week after he left, Ji Ai, with a bundle in hand, went to work in the provincial capital. Nobody could stop her. She said she'd be gone for the summer only. She'd be back to harvest the wheat in autumn.

For fear that she would never get rid of her shame if not let alone, her father consented. In a shirt with red flowers on a green base and a pair of black tights, a long braid slung over each shoulder, she walked barefoot to the county seat holding a pair of new cloth shoes in her hand. As soon as she arrived in town, she put on her shoes, entered a small restaurant where she ate a bowl of noodles, and then went directly to the railway station. Within thirty minutes she was on her way to the provincial capital. Early the next morning, she arrived at the city full of tall buildings and gasoline vehicles—quite different from the county seat. Hu Sheng is here building tall buildings, she said to herself. He is on his way to marrying a crippled woman. Does she wear braids? Is her face white? Does she have round lip corners? Ji Ai had mixed feelings as she left the platform.

Ji Ai had spent one third of the money she'd brought from home. Now she bought a piece of bread to soothe her hunger. She wanted to drink, but she had to pay for water. So she spent twenty *fen* for a cup of tea. Tea and bread obviously could not compare with the well water and new wheat at home, but she didn't want her stomach to suffer, lest it grumble.

With her stomach filled, she felt dizzy no more, though she still had difficulty telling the directions. Where should she go? Who might help her find a job? She was shy of words and she knew nobody in town. So she had to ask whoever looking nice and kind where she might find a job.

Most of the people she asked told her to go to a labor market to see if she could get a job as a baby-sitter. But Ji Ai didn't want to be one. Baby-sitting and cooking were not much different from what she did at home. Working for a family was too small a world for her. She walked slowly along a road, looking at the shops on both sides until she was attracted by the shop front of a particular restaurant. Two strings of red lanterns hung at the gate, with six lanterns on each string resembling sugar-coated hawthorns on a stick, very appealing to the eye. As she looked in a trance, out of the shop came a yellow-haired woman in a purple suit.

"Want to eat? We have rice, dishes, dumplings and steamed buns with stuffing."

Ji Ai tossed her head. "I want a job," she said.

"A part-time job, you mean?" the woman asked excitedly.

"Yes," Ji Ai said, nodding. "I just got off the train."

"Do you wish to work here?" the woman asked. "We're short of hands right now."

Ji Ai thought it over and then followed the woman into the restaurant. The odor of liquor and meat met her nose. The interior of the restaurant was luxurious, looking more splendid than the gate. It was not yet noon, so there were few diners. Up the staircase at the corner was a large glass urn in which were kept snakes and turtles. She was startled by these. She followed the woman in purple to a room upstairs where the woman knocked at the door and a voice from inside answered, "Come in."

As the door opened, Ji Ai saw a large black table shining bright. On a leather swivel chair behind the desk sat a monkey of a man, smoking. His eyes lit up at the sight of her. She carried a bundle under her arm, wore a petticoat with red flowers on a green base, black tights, and black cloth shoes, and she had two thick black braids swung over her shoulders. Her round face shone like a silver plate.

"Manager Li, this girl comes from the countryside," the

woman in purple said. "She wants a job, so I've brought her here."

Manager Li waved the woman away. She left and closed the door behind her. Ji Ai lowered her head and looked at the shoes she was wearing. Against the red carpet they looked even more simple than they did before. She wondered why they'd put such fine covering on the floor rather than on a *kang* (a heatable brick bed). Were their feet really so dear?

"What's your name?" Manager Li asked.

"Ji Ai," she answered, her head lowered. A sudden "click" gave her a start. Raising her head, she saw that Manager Li was lighting a cigarette. The flame leapt up briskly. His thinness reminded her of Hu Sheng's elder brother.

"I'll keep you," Manager Li said slowly. "Four hundred yuan a month, with free board and lodging, and chances of a raise if you do well."

Ji Ai almost dropped her bundle out of joy. She now had a place to eat and live in town. Four hundred yuan a month! What a fortune! But she didn't know what he meant by "doing well." Surely she wouldn't do a bad job!

"What do you mean by a 'raise'?" Ji Ai asked meticulously.

"More money," Manager Li said, laughing.

Ji Ai laughed too, her two round lip corners looming.

Later she changed into a purple suit. Her upper garments and pants were both one size smaller so that her shape looked even rounder. She first tended average clients on the ground floor, serving them drinks and vegetables and clearing the tables. She usually worked until midnight. She lived in the basement of the restaurant with three other waitresses. Two of them were quite urbanized and had no rustic accent, and the cosmetics they used were quite presentable. The first night Ji Ai stayed there a good-looking Wu Jing asked her whether she had any lice.

Ji Ai said no.

"Not even in your hair?" Wu Jing asked.

She answered no. Wu Jing brought out a delicate little bottle containing a green liquid which she sprayed on Ji Ai without a word—to sterilize her, as she later put it. Ji Ai took it for medicine, but it smelt of a strong fragrance.

"Don't panic," Wu Jing said, "it's perfume."

All the customers at the restaurant liked Ji Ai. Because of her diligence she was transferred to work in the private rooms upstairs. She was in charge of the "Elegance Hall" with mahogany tables, chairs and genuine leather couches. The overbearing guests would order all kinds of seafood and even sing sometimes for the fun of it. In Ji Ai's eyes they were there for amusement rather than for food. She would stand at the door for instructions after serving the courses. One time guests asked her to drink with them and she answered by saying that she had "no money for that." The guests burst out laughing and told her she didn't have to pay at all. Well, Ji Ai thought, why should I refuse if I can make you happy by having a drink with you and it doesn't cost me anything? She took the cup and downed it, smiling with her lips compressed. Another time the guests asked her to sing karaoke. She couldn't, so she sang some folk tunes instead, which produced a surprising effect. They clapped their hands loudly to cheer her on. And this made business at the Elegance Hall brisk like a fire for cooking pig heads. A month later, Manager Li raised her monthly pay to five hundred yuan.

With the money in hand Ji Ai thought of going window shopping, visiting a park or seeing some movies. But she had no time

to spare. She had to go to work in the restaurant in the morning
and come back to the basement late at night. By then her legs
would be so sore that she immediately felt like sleeping. If she
was exhausted she would snore. Her friends would stuff her nostrils with their stinking socks, and stifled, she would blink her
eyes, turn over and fall back to snoring again. The other girls
gradually took a liking to Ji Ai because she scoured the floor
clean and even washed their dirty clothes after she arrived. After washing, her hands looked white and tender, the round
whorls at her finger joints as lovely as her lip corners.

Later, Ji Ai found out that Manager Li's name was Li Yingxu.
He lived at the restaurant day and night. His wife was said to be
very wasteful with his money and himself. They were now living
separately. Ji Ai saw Mrs Li sometimes. Even her ankles were
wrapped in gold chains. Her lips were red, as if stained with
chicken blood. Having painted her eyebrows and eyelids, she
looked as if she was always sleepy. Every time she came to the
restaurant she wanted money. So Manager Li gave her money.
Whether he gave her his body or not was something they would
never find out. Anyway, he was a chain smoker and so thin that
he walked without producing any sound at all. After working for
two months at the rate of five hundred yuan a month, Ji Ai
asked Manager Li for a day's leave.

"What do you want to do?" he asked, his face ringed in
smoke.

"I've been in town for two months," Ji Ai murmured, "but I
still don't know what it looks like."

"What do you want to see?"

"I'd like to do some window shopping, have a picture of me
taken in a park and go to the cinema. I've never yet been in a

cinema."

"What else?" Manager Li asked gently.

"I might think of something once I get onto the street," Ji Ai said.

"Okay. You may take a day off," said Manager Li.

"Just deduct a day's pay of mine," Ji Ai said gleefully.

Manager Li did not comment on the suggestion, but said that he'd take a day off too.

Why did he tell me that? Ji Ai wondered. She thanked him and flew to the basement. Shedding her purple suit, she put on the clothes she had worn when she first came to the city: a shirt with red flowers on a green base, black tights and black cloth shoes. They felt tighter than before. She had apparently gained weight. She no longer wore her braids. She wore her hair over shoulders like other girls so that her round face looked prettier.

She took out three hundred yuan from under her pillow where she used to put all the things Hu Sheng had given her. She became a little sad at the thought of him, but soon beat off the feeling. Then she locked the door and went into town.

She was dazzled by the light of the day. She didn't know how to get to the parks or stores, but she decided to go shopping first. She would buy a sleeveless jacket for her father, a coat for her mother, a pair of pants and durable socks for her brother and a short-sleeved shirt for herself. It was so hot. After shopping she would go to a park. However much it cost, she would have a picture taken of herself and, when it was developed, would put it in a mirror frame and show it off to her neighbors. Finally she would go and see a film at the cinema.

As she came to the street corner and was about to ask the way to a shopping center, a red car suddenly stopped right in front of her. Manager Li opened the door and told her to get in.

Ji Ai was given a start. She never knew Manager Li could drive. So this monkey of a man does have something to be proud of, she thought to herself. She hesitated until he urged her, "It's not allowed to stop here. If you don't get in the police will arrive soon and I will have to cut your pay by one month!"

Ji Ai consented. She was quite nervous about her first ride in a car. The car went on its way slowly. "Whose car is it?" she asked after a short while.

"Mine," Manager Li said, looking at her with a smile.

"Your own car?" Ji Ai was puzzled.

Manager Li said that he had brought his camera and was going to take photos of her. "Did you take a day off just to accompany me?" she asked.

"Is that Okay?" Manager Li said, laughing.

Accompany me if you must, Ji Ai thought to herself. Having a car is really convenient. You can go wherever you like. She bought all she wanted to buy for her family before purchasing a pale blue silk short-sleeved shirt for herself. She put it on in the changing room. It was too hot outside. Looking at her round shoulders in the mirror she was pleased with it and came out with her old shirt in hand. "You can be better dressed than that," Manager Li said as he looked at her, smiling.

"This is good enough," Ji Ai responded.

Afterwards they went to a park. Ji Ai posed for photos at an octagonal pavilion, on the quaint bridge and in groves of flowers and green. Manager Li told her to smile every time he took a shot.

She did as she was told and smiled right from her heart, the round lines at her lip corners appearing naturally.

They left the park and headed for a restaurant. In order to save Manager Li's money, Ji Ai only asked for a bowl of noodles with fried sauce, but what appeared on the table was duck in brine and shrimp meat. She enjoyed the meal very much. "Just pay half of my wage this month," she said. "Traffic, food and photography—all this may now add up to several hundred yuan."

Manager Li smiled and asked her if she had a boyfriend.

"Yes and no," she answered gloomily and after much hesitation. "He is getting married here in the city, with a one-legged girl."

"Oh?" Manager Li's face contracted a little and then he asked about her family. After lunch they took their film to be developed and went to see a movie.

By evening they were able to get their photos. Ji Ai smiled at each one of them.

The photos eventually found their way under her pillow. They were enough to fill three mirror frames. Isn't that great? During the day she worked at Elegance Hall in her purple suit. By night she missed her kinsmen, the pigs, the chickens, the courtyard and the small river in her village. She decided to go home for the wheat harvest. She had lived long enough in the city.

Elegance Hall had shining silver plates for famous delicacies. When empty, they emitted a light resembling moonbeams. Ji Ai liked them very much. Every time she held one she felt as if she were holding the moon. A cook told her that the restaurant had a total of a hundred such plates, each costing about seventy yuan.

"It's so expensive," Ji Ai said. "Is it pure silver?"

"Pure silver of such size would cost at least eight hundred

yuan," the cook said. "They're galvanized."

Still, Ji Ai treated them like pure silver. When business was over and the dish washers were busy, she would volunteer to help wash the silver plates. She touched them as if she were touching the soft moonlight and it seemed that a gentle feeling was rising in her. After washing them she would carefully wipe away the water drops with a clean gauze until they shined. She would then stand one before her and look herself in the reflection. Though unable to see her eyes and dimples in it, she could see the round contours of her face just one size smaller.

On pay day Ji Ai discovered that Manager Li had not deducted the costs incurred when they went out together. Being embarrassed about it, she counted out two hundred yuan and went to knock at Manager Li's door. The morose Manager Li was smoking as usual. His face lit up on seeing Ji Ai.

Ji Ai handed the two hundred yuan to him. "This is for the food, the traffic, the photographs and the film tickets," she said.

Manager Li smiled, put the money under the phone and extinguished his cigarette. Ji Ai thought she was right to have returned the money as he had accepted it without the slightest courtesy. She liked his style.

By September, Ji Ai could already smell the mature wheat in her dreams. She decided she would resign and go back for the wheat harvest. She would never come back again because she now knew what urban life was like. People and automobiles everywhere, small living spaces, polluted air.... Hu Sheng was really idiotic to choose to stay in such a filthy place, and with a disabled girl at that! Why wouldn't he rather hang himself with his own necktie?

She went to see Manager Li and said to him smilingly, "It's time I went home for the wheat harvest. I'm not going to work at the restaurant anymore. Please pay me in advance. It's only four days to the end of a month. Pay me a hundred yuan less."

Manager Li's face sank. After a long silence he lit another cigarette, stared at Ji Ai's silver-plate face and asked her in a suppressed voice, "Will you come back again?"

"No."

"Why?"

"I just don't want to."

"I won't let you go."

"But I must," Ji Ai insisted.

"How much does your wheat cost?" Manager Li said menacingly, "I can pay for it."

"It's not a matter of money," Ji Ai replied, "I miss the wheat."

Though she failed to get paid, her decision to go home did not change. She had already packed. However, she thought it unfair that she should get nothing for nearly a month's work. Late one night she stole into the kitchen and took six silver plates out of the glass cabinet. She thought they would serve as her pay. And she loved the silver plates.

She dressed herself in her usual attire of red-flowered shirt, black tights and black shoes. For fear that she might frighten her parents by wearing her hair loose she plaited it into two long braids again. Packing the six silver plates into her bundle, she went on her way home. As she left the city by train she felt no regrets at all. The next day she arrived at the county seat. The fairs on the first and fifteenth of every lunar month made her feel that life here was better than it was in the city. After eating something, she found herself walking barefoot on the country road with her shoes in hand. This time she felt the country was again better than the county seat.

She had not gone barefoot for an entire summer. No wonder she found blisters on the soles of her feet when she arrived at her home. The family was overjoyed to see her. Her mother brought a basin of water for her to soak her feet in. "Has Hu Sheng found you, Ji Ai?" her mother asked quietly.

"Why should he look for me?" Ji Ai said, pursing up her lips.

"He came back several days ago," her mother replied. "He wanted to see you, but went back after he heard you were in the city."

Ji Ai was silent.

"He isn't married yet," her mother continued. "He said he kept thinking of you the day he went to register for marriage. In the end he dropped the idea of applying for a marriage certificate."

Ji Ai was now on the point of tears.

"He was laid off by the contract team. He's coming back to farm."

"Why did he go back to the provincial capital again?" Ji Ai asked.

"To look for you," her mother answered. "He said he'd come back for the harvest as soon as he found you."

Ji Ai started wailing.

Three days later the wheat harvest began. Ji Ai went to the fields with a silver plate in hand. On it she put refreshments. The bright sun endowed the plate with dazzling beauty. Many people came around and showered praises over it. But before the wheat was fully harvested, a police car took her back to the provincial capital again. Manager Li had sued her for the theft of the six silver plates. She pleaded not guilty, claiming that the plates were part of her wages. She didn't even know what crime she had committed. The city became more detestable in her eyes. When the police took the six silver plates out of her room they saw three mirror frames of her color photos full of broad smiles.

By the end of the year she was sentenced to six months at a labor reform farm ten kilometers away from the city. She felt it very inadvisable to have submitted herself to such humiliation for so petty a misdemeanor. The wardens taught the prisoners some law basics and Ji Ai started to repent for what she had done. But still she couldn't figure out why it was wrong to take the silver plates as compensation for payment due. Was it right for her to return home without being paid?

"You ought to have sued him for not paying you," the wardens told her. "You should have acted according to the law."

Ji Ai was still confused. She thought she would never understand.

One week after she was sent to the reform farm someone came to see her. It was Manager Li! Clad in a rice-colored cloak, he looked even thinner than before.

"Ji Ai—" Manager Li cried hoarsely.

"Why do you come to see me after prosecuting me?" Ji Ai asked pathetically. "I couldn't even finish the wheat harvesting."

"I just wanted them to bring you back to the city," Manager Li said, clearing his throat and looking affectionately at her. "I'll marry you when you're released."

Ji Ai was speechless.

"I'm divorced now," Manager Li said. "I gave her three hundred thousand yuan."

"What about the restaurant?" Ji Ai asked.

"It's still mine," said Manager Li.

"That's good," Ji Ai said. "The hen will always lay eggs."

"So you agree to marry me?"

Ji Ai smiled, her two lip corners turning round. "I can't marry you," she said. "I don't like thin people. Hu Sheng's elder brother is as thin as you. After years of marriage he still doesn't have a child. I like having babies."

Looking at Ji Ai, Manager Li was overwhelmed by her purity. "I must marry you," he said.

After that, Manager Li drove there every weekend to see her. Ji Ai turned away at the very sight of him. She never accepted the chocolates and refreshments he intended to give her. She said she was eating better here than in the countryside.

One winter afternoon someone else came to see her. It was Hu Sheng!

Hu Sheng was wearing cloth clothes and a pair of black cloth shoes that Ji Ai had made for him. He looked tearfully at Ji Ai as if he wanted to say he was sorry or something else sweet, but he said nothing. He was waiting for her to give him a slap in the face or a good dressing down, but she only cackled with laughter.

"Why do you laugh?" Hu Sheng asked.

"It's strange that you'd rather have me wait six months here for nothing than marry me. How many things could I have done had I stayed home these six months?"

Hu Sheng's heart was now balanced. He looked affectionately at the woman with a face resembling a silver plate. "I'll take you home to be my bride when your six months are over," he said.

"I've already served more than two months. In three months I will be released," Ji Ai said. "It's time you started preparing for the wedding."

"What would you like?" asked Hu Sheng.

"Six silver plates," Ji Ai replied, her eyes wet.

Translated by Wang Chiying

Bathing in Clean Water

IN Tianzao's view, bathing before the New Year was not so different from shaving bristles off a dead pig. When thick, hard bristles were shaved, a pig would reveal its white, tender skin. Similarly, when a person washed dirt off his or her body, the skin would also look fair and tender. The difference was that the pig would be sliced into pieces and become delicious food for human beings.

People of the Lizhen Township set the 27th day of the 12th month of the lunar calendar as a date of "water discharging." The so-called "water discharging" meant taking a bath. In the Zheng family, Tianzao was responsible for boiling water and throwing it away after use on that day. When he was as young as eight, he began this duty. Already, it had been five years since his appointment.

People in that township took only one bath in a whole year, which occurred on the 27th day of the 12th month. Although women and girls who were fond of cleanliness washed themselves occasionally, that practice was nothing compared with a real bath. In summer, for instance, a woman would wash her feet and legs in a pond on her way home from farming in the fields. A girl would wash her neck and armpits after washing her hair. But the napes and bellies of those bare-backed boys in the height of summer were black, as though covered with bats.

Tianzao's room served temporarily as a "bathroom" during that time. The fire-heated wall of his room was very warm, the curtain long since having been drawn. The order in which they took baths in his family was chronological—from the elderly to the young: Grandma first, then his parents and, finally, the children. Before Grandpa died, he had been the first. He had been very quick. Fifteen minutes would do. And his bath water was not dirty at all. To save water, Tianzao would quickly dip into that water. When someone took a bath, the door would be tightly shut and the door curtain would be lowered. When Tianzao was bathing, his mother would ask, while knocking at the door, "Sonny, shall I help clean your back?"

"No need," Tianzao would reply, curling up in the bathtub like a fish.

"You won't be able to wash yourself clean on your own," Mother would say.

"Why not?" the child would argue. He would splash with his fingers stirring the water, as though to tell his mother that he was working very hard at cleaning himself.

"Don't be shy!" Mother would say, smiling. "You're borne by me. Are you afraid of being seen by your own mother?"

Tianzao would close his legs subconsciously in the tub. Red-faced, he would shout, "What are you talking about? I don't need your help. Don't you hear me!?"

Tianzao had never had a tub of really clean water for a bath. He had to boil water at the oven, throw away the dirty bath water, bucket by bucket, for each family member. So he had to adjust his time to take a quick bath with another's bath water. It was not agreeable at all. To him, it was only a ritual. No matter how clean the bath water was after being used by someone else, he found it murky. So he would sit in the bathtub for some ten minutes, scrubbing off dirt here and there, until he finished the whole business. He hated using his room as a "bathroom," which made the air damp, covering the bulb with dewy beads. At night as he slept, he felt as though he were in a pigsty. So, shortly before the New Year, he stated to Mother, "We should use Tianyun's room as the 'bathroom' this year."

Upon hearing this, Tianyun, who was making a paper flower, craned her neck and said angrily, "Why in my room?"

"Why should mine be used as a 'bathroom' every year?" Tianzao retorted in the same manner.

"You are a boy. A girl's room should not be dirtied," she said indignantly. "Besides, you're a few years older than me. You are my elder brother and you should give way!"

Tianzao stopped arguing. However, he murmured, "I hate the New Year! What's so good about the New Year?"

This made everyone laugh. Since Grandpa had left this world, Grandma rarely smiled. Sometimes, when everyone was doubled up with laughter, she showed no expression, so people assumed that she was hard of hearing. Presently, she broke into laughter, too, on hearing Tianzao's complaint. As she was laughing, some phlegm blocked her windpipe. She coughed so violently that she spat out her false teeth.

It was true that Tianzao did not like the New Year. In the first place, he was not keen on all those rituals, such as burning imitation paper money for the dead, kowtowing to each other and visiting one another to offer blessings. At the junction, the pristine snow on the ground had become filthy because of burning imitation paper money. They looked like scattered dog droppings. A gloom seemed to dominate the New Year. Second, he found the preparations for the New Year tedious. It simply exhausted one, adding aches and pains all over, and brought about grievances: to remove sewn covers from quilts, to whitewash walls, to make paper lanterns, to tailor new clothes, to steam kneaded dough for the New Year cakes, and so on. Everybody, old and young, was involved. Not only did the house need a thorough cleaning, but people, too, had to clean themselves. The 27th day of the 12th month of the lunar calendar was a day for bathing. In the bath, all family members had to scrub off all the dirt from their bodies that had accumulated for a whole year. As a result, everyone appeared to suffer from dropsy. This invariably reminded him of a butcher scraping bristles off a dead pig with an iron brush. He was sick of it. Third, he did not like to see all the people in their new clothes. The new clothes made them look stiff and ridiculous. If they stood in a line, Tianzao thought, they would look like rigidly packed bolts of cloth on fabric store shelves. What he could not tolerate was that the New Year arrived at midnight, when he was at his most sleepy and tired state. He had no appetite, yet he had to boost himself up and eat the New Year dumplings. He was bored to death by all of this. He had often imagined the first thing he would do if he had all the power: change the date of the New Year.

Grandma was the first to finish her bath. Helped by Tianzao's mother, she tottered out of the "bathroom." He spotted the wet, gray hair dangling over her shoulders; the bags under her eyes made her high cheekbones look as though they were ready to drop any minute. The dark age spots on her face appeared darker because of the warm steam, reminiscent of dark clouds before a thunderstorm. Tianzao found his grandma more obese and clumsy, just like a rotten mushroom. He was not sure if all people would be like her when they became old. Grandma, panting, passed through the kitchen and returned to her own room. On seeing Tianzao, she said, "The water you've boiled was very hot. I've had a good bath. My fatigue of the whole year is all gone. You may have a bath using the bath water I've left."

"Grandma has not left this house even once in a whole year," said Mother, "she was not dirty at all. The water is quite clean indeed."

Tianzao said nothing. He threw more firewood into the oven. Then he lifted a bucket and entered his own room. The sultry and steamy air lingered like a mangy dog running about in the room. The bulb was surely covered with roe-like beads of water. With an effort, he lifted the large bathtub and poured its water into the bucket. Wiping perspiration off his forehead, he lifted the bucket and went out. As he passed the kitchen, he met Grandma, who had not returned to her own room yet. She gaped at seeing Tianzao carrying a bucketful of her bath water, her eyes filled with disappointment.

"So you think the water I've used is..." she faltered.

Tianzao was silent. He pulled the door open and went outside. It was dark and cold. With unsteady steps, he carried the water to a drainage ditch outside the entrance gate. In winter, a large, dirty ice mound used to form by the ditch. Many boys were fond of "whipping" tops in the ditch beside the ice mound. They whipped tops hard. Some were so fascinated that they ignored their runny noses. During the day, they enjoyed this activity, and they could not resist playing in the moonlight, too. So they came out of their houses, wearing heavy, cotton-padded coats, and whipped tops. At night in deep winter, one could hear the clear sound of "thud, thud..."

Tianzao spotted a short figure standing on the snowy ground near the ice mound. The figure was bent over a little, as if searching for something, a flickering cigarette held between fingers.

"Tianzao," the figure spoke, standing straight, "out to throw away bath water?"

From the voice, Tianzao recognized one of his classmates, Xiao Dawei, who lived in the next alley. He made an effort to lift the bucket onto the ice mound. "What are you doing here?"

"I whipped a top at dusk and I hit it so hard that I lost sight of it. I just can't find it."

"How can you find it without a flashlight?" As he was asking, he poured the dirty bath water onto the ice mound.

"The bath water smells awful," Dawei said loudly. "Your grandma must have used the water."

"So what?" said Tianzao. "I bet the water used by your grandpa smells even worse."

Dawei's grandpa was bedridden, paralyzed. He needed someone to look after him, even when he relieved himself. Dawei's mother had waited on him from the time when all her hair had been black until it had all turned gray. She complained that she would not want to continue being a filial daughter-in-law and threatened to leave for good. For that remark, her husband had used Dawei's whip, which was normally used for whipping a top, to lacerate her body all over. That became a township scandal.

"Whose dirty bath water did you use for a bath this year?" asked Dawei, obviously annoyed. "I'm always the first to take the bath every year and I always have a whole tub of clean water for myself." He challenged Tianzao.

"I have a tub of clean water of my own, too," protested Tianzao righteously.

"You're boasting!" said Dawei. "You're the one who boils all the water for the family's bath every year. And you always use dirty water to bathe yourself. Is there anyone who doesn't know this?"

"I'll tell your father you're smoking!" Tianzao did not know how to counterattack.

"I only use the light from the cigarette to find my top. I'm not doing anything bad. Go tell him. Let's see if it works."

The irritated boy held the bucket and went home. After a long distance, he turned and shouted towards Dawei, "I will have clean water for a bath this year!"

He looked up and found that the galaxy seemed brighter and was cascading clear water onto him, washing away all his frustration.

Grandma's weeping came from the house. It sounded remote and hollow, reminding one of dripping water in a deep cave.

Tianzao pulled the vat lid open and ladled hot water into the large bathtub. Father stepped over. "What have you done? You've made Grandma sad."

Instead of answering, Tianzao poured cold water into the bathtub. Then he tested it with his hand to see if it was all right. Slightly cold, but just right for his father, Tianzao thought, because he did not like hot water for a bath. If it had been for Tianyun or Mother, he would have had to add more hot water.

"Whose turn next?" Tianzao asked.

"I'll be next," replied Father. "Your mother has to keep your grandma company for a while."

Tianyun dashed out of her room suddenly, wearing only a blue floral vest, revealing her plump arms. Her hair was loose and her eyes were shining. "Let me take a bath first!"

"I'll be very brief," said Father.

"I've already freed my pigtails." With that, she shook her head left and right, her hair billowing up and down. Then she remarked to Father matter-of-factly, "From now on, I must wash before you. What if I use the bathtub you've just used and get pregnant? Who would be responsible for the consequence?"

This made Father double up with laughter and spit out phlegm. Tianzao laughed, too, throwing down the ladle. Tianyun pursed her little, full lips, her face glowing like the fire in the oven.

"Who on earth has told you that you'll get pregnant just because you use the bathtub Dad has used for a bath?" Father asked, chortling.

"I was just told. Don't press me for that."

Tianyun soon gave her instructions to Tianzao, "I'll wash my hair first. Give me a basin of lukewarm water. I want that blue fragrant shampoo of Mother's, too!"

Tianyun's careless words chased away all of Tianzao's gloominess. He was glad to serve his younger sister. When he was about to scoop water into the basin, Tianyun stamped her foot and cried, "Oh no! That basin is too dirty. Clean it up or I won't wash my hair."

"It's quite clean, isn't it?" said Father jokingly.

"Just have a good look at it! There's a ring of slime on the edge, just as obvious as the dark circles around Widow Snake's eyes. How can you say it's clean?" the girl argued, her face outlined with contempt.

The surname of this Widow Snake was Cheng. Since she liked to flirt with men in the town, women said, behind her back, that she was the incarnation of a poisonous snake. As time went on, she was nicknamed Widow Snake. She walked with her hand pounding her back. She had no children, and life was easy and leisurely. She rose late and her eyes were permanently ringed with dark circles. People wondered if she lacked sleep. She was fond of little girls, and little girls liked to rummage through her trunks and talk her into giving them hair accessories that she had used in her young days.

"Ah, I see," said Father, "it must be that Widow Snake who told you about pregnancy. That slut!"

"How can you say such a thing? Shame on you!" cried Tianyun.

Tianzao meant to use soap to wash away the slime, but Tianyun insisted that he used soda powder. He had to fetch it in the kitchen cabinet. However, he could not help saying, "What a fussy girl! All you've got is mousy hair."

The girl quickly picked up a few soya beans and threw them at him, yelling, "It's you who has mousy hair!" After a second, she continued, "We have only one New Year in a whole year. If I don't wash my hair clean, how can I use the new ribbon to tie it up?"

As they chatted and laughed in the kitchen, the weeping of the old woman drifted over.

"Why is she crying?" queried Tianyun.

Father glanced at Tianzao. "It's all your brother's fault. He refused to use the water Grandma had used. She is very hurt. I bet she'll be in low spirits this New Year."

"But will she give me New Year gift money?* If not, I'll tear up all of Tianzao's textbooks so that he can't do his homework for the winter vacation. He will surely be scolded for that by his school masters when school begins."

When they were amiable, the girl called Tianzao "brother." If she was upset at him, she used his name.

By then, Tianzao had washed the basin clean. "If you dare tear up my textbooks, I'll cut your new hair ribbon into pieces, so that you'll have nothing to tie up your mousy pigtails."

"How dare you!" Tianyun gritted her teeth.

While scooping water into the basin, Tianzao said, "Okay, see if I dare or don't dare."

With tears in her eyes, she turned to her father and whined, "Dad, Tianzao's bullying me!"

"I dare him!" said Father, holding up his palm over Tianzao's head. "I'll kick him out if he does!"

Tianzao carried the basin and then the tub into his small room. Tianyun wanted more clean water for her hair, so Tianzao prepared enough water for two basins. She complained again, saying that the curtain was not properly drawn. "What if someone sees me bathing?" Tianzao had to adjust the curtain until the window was tightly covered. Like a servant, he obedient-

---

* On the eve of the lunar New Year, the elders give children red paper bags containing cash.

ly brought her a towel, a comb, slippers, shampoo and fragrant soap. Only then did Tianyun enter the room with the air of a queen and shut the door. About three minutes later came the sounds of splashing water.

Father went to the storeroom to find a pair of red plastic palace lanterns. After a whole year of storage, they must be dusty. The family elders liked to use Tianyun's bath water to wash the lanterns, as though she were linked with splendor and brightness.

Tianzao filled up the pot and threw more firewood into the oven. Then he left the kitchen and went quietly to Grandma's bedroom door to eavesdrop.

Grandma sniveled, "In those days, I was the cleanest in the village. Everybody knew that. If I jumped into a river to take a bath, the fish would hide. Fish lived in the water every day but knew that they were not as fair-complexioned as me, not as clean as me..."

Tianzao could not help stifling a chuckle.

Then he heard Mother console her, "The boy should know better. However, it's not worth getting upset with him. You are fond of cleanliness. It is known to all in this town. Take the bean paste you've made, for example. All the neighbors like it. Apart from its good taste, it is clean."

Grandma grinned and then said, sadly, "My hair is forever free of fleas. There is no smell in my armpits, nor any dirt under my toenails. The water I have used for a bath can be used to water peonies."

Grandma's thought was so absurd that even Mother could not help chuckling. Tianzao rushed back to the oven and guffawed in front of the leaping flames. Presently, Father came in with a gust of cold air, holding two old palace lanterns. His face was covered with dust, his nose runny, unseemly for his age. He was indeed the image of a scavenger. Noticing Tianzao's mirth, he asked, "What's so funny, sonny?"

Tianzao repeated what he had heard.

Father put down the lanterns and laughed, "She's just an old child!"

The water in the pot was roaring with bubbles, as though the oven was scorching summer and inside the pot were a horde of cicadas crying with all their might, "It's too hot! It's too hot!" The flame roasted Tianzao's cheeks. He went to the window and pressed his face against a frosty pane. He felt a sudden pang of cold needles tattooing his face. Then he discovered that one of his cheeks was numb. When he moved away from the pane, he saw a crescent print on the glass. He wiped his wet cheek and looked through the transparent part of the glass. It was black outside and he could see nothing in the courtyard. Only the stars in the sky reflected dim light. Tianzao heaved a sigh, looked away in disappointment and turned to look at the oven fire. Just as he squatted down, the door opened and in burst cold air. A woman stood there in a green satin padded coat, her eyes rimmed with dark circles.

She asked Tianzao loudly, " 'Water-discharging,' eh?"

"Yeah." Tianzao, seeing that it was Widow Snake, replied reluctantly.

"Is your dad home?" She withdrew her hands from her pockets, wiped off her nasal mucus and cleaned her fingers on one of her shoes. Tianzao felt like vomiting.

Hearing her voice, Tianzao's father came over.

"Brother, do me a favor, please," she said. "I've just got

bath water ready, but found something wrong with my tub. It was leaking when I poured water into it."

"Why?" asked Father.

"Last autumn, I put dried beans in that tub to remove their husks. The husks were so dry and hard, which hurt my hands. Seeing that my hands were almost bleeding, I used a pine rod to pound the beans. Who knew that it would crack the tub? I did not know at the time."

Tianzao's mother came out, too. "Oh!" she uttered in surprise, upon seeing Widow Snake. Then she added, unenthusiastically, "So, you are here."

Widow Snake greeted Mother simply, too. Then she fished out a red silk ribbon from a sleeve. "This is for Tianyun."

Seeing that his parents did not take it, Tianzao did not respond, either. So the woman lay the ribbon on the lid of the vat, which made it look like a wedding present.

"Where's Tianyun?" she asked.

"She's having a bath," replied Mother.

"Do you have any tin metal at home?" Father asked.

Before she could answer, Mother interrupted, "What do you need tin for?"

"My tub is leaking. I begged Tianzao's father to repair it," Widow Snake answered. Then she turned to the man. "No, I don't."

"It can't be done then," said Father, who then had a good excuse for not helping her.

"A basin will do," said Tianzao's mother.

Her eyes opened wide, the woman shook her head and said, "That won't do. We have one New Year in a whole year, haven't we? It must not be neglected." That was exactly what

Tianyun had said.

"If you don't have any tin, I don't know how to help you."
Tianyun's father furrowed his brow and continued, "Perhaps
you might try asphalt felt. Tear a piece of it, burn it over a fire
until it drips oil. Cover the crack evenly with the oil. When it
gets cold, the crack may seal."

"Oh please, it's better if you do it for me." She always looked
guileless in front of men. "I can't understand what you are saying..."

Tianzao's father glanced at his wife. In fact, it was no use.
No matter what expression she wore to indicate agreement or
disagreement, she was set against it in her heart. But when everyone turned his or her eyes to her for her decision, she had to
say loudly, "Go ahead, then."

With a "thanks," Widow Snake left, followed by Tianzao's
father. Before he shut the door, he turned to look at his wife a-
gain. She glared at him and spat out a mouthful of phlegm. The
glare punctuated by the phlegm turned into a big exclamation
mark, which made the husband shudder as he crossed the threshold. While walking in the cold wind, he said to himself that he
had to hurry and return home as quickly as possible. He warned
himself not to drink tea or smoke cigarettes offered by Widow
Snake. He had to return in the same state as he had left.

"Tianyun is such a nuisance," said Mother. "If not for her,
Widow Snake wouldn't have come." After Widow Snake left,
she became absent-minded. She carried a small basin in which to
knead dough but forgot to mix yeast in the dough.

"Why did you agree to let Father go?" Tianzao deliberately
baited her. "She might cook two dishes and drink wine with Father."

"How dare she!" Mother said angrily. "If that's the case, I won't clean his back."

"He can do that himself. He's a grown-up. Is it necessary to help clean his back every year, eh?"

Mother flushed and then said tersely, "Better go and boil your water. It's not child's business."

Tianzao became silent. The flames in the oven were licking the black bottom of the pot with their little golden tongues, which made the water cry noisily. Illuminated by the flames and enveloped in steam, Tianzao felt drowsy. Still squatting before the oven, he began to nod off. But, before long, he was awakened by Tianyun's wet hand. He opened his eyes and noticed that she had already finished bathing, her face aglow, her hair wet and free. She was in new cotton knitwear, a sweet smell emitting from her body. "I've finished bathing," she said buoyantly.

"Okay, you've finished bathing. So what?" Tianzao said languidly, rubbing his eyes.

"You can take your bath with the water I've used."

"Of course not," retorted Tianzao. "You are just like a big, stinking fish. The water you've used smells awful."

Mother had just finished the kneading and left the dough on the heated *kang*.* As she emerged, Tianyun whimpered, "Mom, Tianzao's bullying me again. He called me a big, stinking fish."

"I'll sew up his lips if he dares say it again," threatened Mother, miming an act of sewing threateningly.

Whenever he bickered with her sister, Tianzao knew that his

---

* A heatable brick bed.

parents would always side with her. He got used to it and was not upset. Instead, he lifted the two lanterns into the "bathroom" to clean them. Presently, he heard Tianyun crying in delight, "That ribbon on the vat is for me, isn't it? It's gorgeous!"

The lanterns were of hard plastic. Due to the long years of natural wear, the plastic was aging and had shrunk. They no longer looked round and full. Besides, the red had already faded. The middle section was actually pale because of the light. Nothing was joyful about them. So the family had to use red bulbs or else the lanterns would be pale green, compromising the atmosphere of the New Year. While brushing the lanterns clean, Tianzao pondered over all of the New Year's complicated formalities that annoyed him. He blurted, "What's good about the New Year?" The only reply to his question was the moist air, which permeated the whole room. Irritated, he cried, "I will move the New Year to June so that everybody can bathe in the river."

After cleaning the lanterns, he carried the dirty water, one bucket at a time, to dump outside. But, he saw no sign of Dawei near the ice mount. Tianzao wondered if he had found his top. The evening was no longer young. As it had deepened, the stars could hardly be seen. Their weak light reminded one of a dying man's last breath. Tianzao looked up, but one glance was enough because the starlight was swallowed by the darkness. It was too gloomy a sight. The biting cold was so unbearable that he had to go back to the house.

Father was not back yet. Mother looked anxious. It was her turn to bathe. Tianzao cleaned the bathtub for her and poured in the hot water. Mother gazed at the steam spiraling up from the tub as if expecting a marmalade to leap out of the water, but in vain.

"Mom, the water is ready," Tianzao reminded her.

"Oh." Sighing deeply, she remarked, "Why isn't your father back? Perhaps you should go to Widow Snake's house."

Tianzao pretended not to understand her real meaning. "No, I won't. Father is an adult. Surely he will not get lost. Besides, I have to boil water. You'd better go yourself."

"Of course not," huffed Mother. "Who is she, after all?"

She seemed to regain her composure and raised her voice, "When your father and I were courting, a teacher was pursuing me. However, I ignored him. I was deeply in love with your father, though he was only a mason."

"But why didn't you marry the teacher then?" Tianzao goaded her. "If that had been the case, I could've studied at home."

"If that had been the case, you wouldn't have come into this world." Mother could not help laughing, finally. "Now, I've got to take a bath or the water will get cold."

Refreshed and clean, Tianyun was trying on her new clothes in her own small room. Tianzao heard her singing, "A little doggy rolls out its little tongue to lick the picture book in my hand. There's a little doggy in the picture book, too. It is sleeping in the sunshine."

Tianyun was fond of composing her own songs. When she was high-spirited, her songs were compassionate and cheerful. When she was unhappy, her songs were militant and vigorous. Once, she had used a duster for cleaning and brushed a vase off the table. It had shattered. For that, Mother had scolded her. Not willing to submit, she had returned to her room and composed a song, "The duster is a big gray wolf. The vase is a little lamb. 'I'm starved, for I've not eaten anything for three days and nights. How can I let you go?'" Her point had been that the little lamb (the vase) should be eaten. Why didn't it run away in the first place since it had legs? Her song had made everyone laugh and think that, indeed, it was unnecessary to wrong the girl just because of a little vase. So someone had said, "It is time that the vase broke. It is so old and no one looks at it." The sullen little girl had broken into a smile.

Tianzao filled up the vat again and poked at the burning firewood, stirring up a shower of golden sparks, just like a blowing dandelion. Then he threw in two thick pieces of pinewood. Grandma soon tottered out, her hair already dried, but still loosened instead of in a bun. This made her look awful. She was bulky; her eyes, puffy. Normally, her eyes were like green grapes. But today they seemed like a pair of red lanterns because of her weeping. Those dark age spots on her face were like withered leaves pasted on her face. Tianzao wanted to tell her that only thick, black hair would look good loosened over the shoulders. Anyone with straggly, gray and thin hair loosened over her shoulders would look ridiculous. But, on second thought, he held back, for he did not want to upset her again. So he lowered his head and busied himself with tending the fire.

"Tianzao," Grandma said in grief and anger, "am I really an eyesore to you? You threw away the water I had used. You don't even bother to look at me when I stand in front of you."

Tianzao neither answered nor looked up.

"You want to spoil my New Year, right?" Her tone became more doleful.

"No," said Tianzao. "All I want is to take a bath with clean water, not the water used by someone else. I didn't use the bath water Tianyun had used, either." While speaking, he kept his head down.

"The water used by Tianyun should be used for washing the lanterns," she argued childishly.

"Mom will finish her bath soon. I won't use her bath water either." Tianzao was adamant.

"What about your dad's?" Grandma wouldn't give up.

"No, I won't use it," Tianzao said determinedly.

Grandma became amiable. "Tianzao, everyone will grow old. You're now a child with fair and tender skin. But sooner or later, that skin of yours will grow loose and shriveled. Am I right?"

To make Grandma leave quickly, Tianzao lifted his head and said tersely, "Yes."

"When I was your age, I was much lovelier than you," said Grandma. "I was as tender and fresh as the first new shoots of spring onion out of the earth."

"Sure," said Tianzao. "When I am as old as you, I bet I won't be as young-looking as you. My back will be so hunched that my head will almost touch the ground. My face will be dotted with a fungal disease, like favus."

Grandma chuckled. But soon she realized that her grandson had painted too terrible a picture for his future. So she said, "Only a mangy dog suffers from favus. How can a man grow favus? If anyone suffers from favus, he would have to be heartless. Anyway, as long as you know that everyone will be old, that's enough. Don't curse yourself!"

"Yeah…"

Grandma began to ask if the lanterns were washed clean; if the soya beans, which would be panned, were soaking in water. Then she touched the lid of the water vat and found some slime

on it. So she began a tirade at others for being lazy. There was
no festival atmosphere, she concluded. After this, she began
reminiscing about how people had celebrated the New Year in
her young days. In one phrase, the celebration had been neat,
clean and prosperous. Finally, she felt thirsty and, with a sigh,
had to return to her room. She kept coughing. On hearing that,
Tianzao knew that she was about to sleep. Every night before
going to bed, she would cough thoroughly in order to clear her
throat. Only then would she fall asleep peacefully. Predictably,
when the coughing stopped, the light in her room went out.

Tianzao sighed deeply in relief.

Mother used to take a long bath in the past. It took at least
one hour. One had to soak thoroughly in water first, she said.
Only then could all the dirt be scrubbed off his body. But, this
year, in only half an hour, she emerged from the "bathroom."
As soon as she saw Tianzao, she asked anxiously, "Isn't your
dad back yet?"

"No."

"It's been a long time," Mother said worriedly. "Ten bathtubs
could have been repaired."

Just as Tianzao lifted the bucket of Mother's water to dump
outside, she said, "Your dad has not come back yet. My bath
was brief this year. Why don't you use the water for a bath
now?"

"No," was Tianzao's resolute answer.

Mother glanced at him in surprise. "In that case, I'll wash
some clothes in the water. It would be a pity to throw it away."

Mother took two items of clothing to wash. Tianzao could
hear the sharp noise of the clothes being rubbed against a wash-
board. It sounded like a hungry pig's grunts at the trough. If Fa-

ther had not come home in time, the clothes would have been rubbed to rags.

It was lucky for these two pieces of clothing. As they were groaning, Father pushed the door open and entered with a gust of cold wind. He looked flustered, his face covered with black soot and dust.

"Should be my turn, right?" he asked Tianzao.

"Yes," Tianzao replied. Mother came out, her hands covered with soap bubbles. Seeing her husband, she raised her eyebrows and said, "Well, it's been ages since you left to repair the tub and what you've got is a face of dust. Leakage mended?"

"Mended," Father faltered.

"Well done." She spat out the words through gritted teeth.

"Well done," Father replied, puzzled.

"Bah!" Mother grunted. Father added hastily, his face growing red, "I mean, the bathtub's leakage was well mended."

"Didn't she reward you with a basin of water to clean your face?" Mother said sarcastically.

Father wiped his face with his hands. Since his hands had more soot, his face became even dirtier. "All I did was repair that bathtub of hers," he said, feeling very much wronged, "I didn't have a sip of her tea, or a cigarette. I didn't dare wash my face in her place."

"Well, anxious to come home, eh?" said Mother. "Where on earth did you get all the soot on your face? Did you crawl beneath her *kang*?"

Like a child caught in a heinous act, Father stood straight, not moving from his spot, as if talking to a parent, not his wife. He babbled, "As soon as I entered her house, I was choked by smoke and tears kept running down my face. A pitiful woman, indeed. For three years, she had not cleaned the smoke shaft. Fire was needed everyday. Naturally, the wall of the smoke shaft was covered with soot and dust. Whenever the oven was used, smoke was discharged. Who can bear that? No wonder her eyes are always black. Life is not easy for a widow. So, after mending the bathtub, I helped in cleaning the smoke shaft."

"But how can you clean it while it's hot?" Mother was suspicious.

"That's why all I could do was to remove three bricks and rake out some soot. Anyway, the shaft is unblocked now. Let her pass the New Year first. When spring comes, I'll do a thorough cleaning for her." The man stupidly confessed to what was on his mind.

"A lucky star shines over her." Feigning a smile, Mother continued, "So she has a helping hand, free of charge."

With that, she asked Tianzao to throw away her bath water since she had finished washing the clothes. Tianzao carried out the bucket of dirty water and skirted around his father, who was still standing there with his heart pounding. When he returned, he saw that Father had washed his face, but the water in the basin was as black as if cuttlefish had frolicked in it. Mother glanced over and said, "Tianzao may take the water to school to 'blackwash' the blackboard."

"Oh, come on. Can't you say something nice? I just helped her a little."

"Did I say you should not help her?" Mother retorted, overcome with jealousy. "In fact, I would not object if you moved in with her."

Father was silent. He knew it was no use arguing with her now. Tianzao hurriedly prepared bath water for him, thinking that once his father entered the "bathroom" to take his bath, Mother's resentment would cease and Father would be relieved of being embarrassed further. Indeed, when a bathtub of clean, lukewarm water was ready in Tianzao's room, Mother took the clothing and went out. When Father was about to shut the door, he said to her, "Help me clean my back, will you?"

"Do it yourself," replied Mother, still smarting from the unhappy event.

Tianzao could not help laughing secretly. Father was truly pitiful. All he did was help that widow a little. For that, he had to be so docile at home. In the past, when Father had taken a bath, Mother would enter the "bathroom" to help him clean his back. Apparently, Father would not enjoy such treatment this year.

Tianzao filled up the pot again, and then enthusiastically threw more firewood into the oven. "Why are you boiling more water?" Mother stepped over and asked.

"For my bath."

"Aren't you going to use your father's bath water?"

"I want clean water," Tianzao stressed.

Mother said nothing and entered Tianyun's room. Tianzao did not hear anything from that room. Usually, once Mother entered Tianyun's room, the girl would babble ceaselessly like a summer frog croaking by a pond. But, unexpectedly, the light in Tianyun's room was switched off. As he puzzled over this, his mother came out. "What a girl, sleeping with a ribbon in her hand! She only covered her legs with the quilt, leaving her belly uncovered. What if she catches cold and diarrhea in the middle of the night? Besides, she forgot to switch off the light. The New Year makes her too excited and fatigues her."

Tianzao smiled. He poked at the burning firewood and again saw the dancing golden sparks. To him, the oven was a night sky and the sparks were the stars. The little world there always filled people with warmth.

The water in the pot began to sing buoyantly. Firewood crackled. Mother returned to the bed room where she and Tianzao's father shared and folded up clothes that had been washed two days before. Obviously her mind was troubled, because she poked her head out and asked Tianzao "what was that noise?" every few minutes.

"Nothing," Tianzao said finally.

"But I heard a sound... Isn't your dad calling me?"

"No."

Disappointed, she withdrew her head. But, before long, she poked her head out and asked again, "What is it, the sound?" Her hand held the same folded clothes that she had held when she had asked the same question before.

At last, Tianzao knew what was on her mind. So he said, "It's Dad, calling you."

"Calling me?" Her eyes lit up for a second. Then she shook her head. "Forget it."

"He's unable to clean his back." Tianzao knew that Mother was expecting his encouragement. "He will get the new vest dirty the first day he wears it."

"Have to pay him for what I owed him in my last life," mumbled Mother. With a sigh, she happily put down the clothes and entered the "bathroom." Tianzao heard her complaining at first, then found her voice warming up, though still rebuking Father. Finally, her voice became very soft. Later, the soft talking ceased. He could only hear the crisp sound of splashing water. It was so agreeable, his heart was tickled. He felt his face getting very hot; the fire made him very sleepy. He took a piece of wood and put it under his seat, cupped his head in his hands and dozed off. As he was about to dream, he heard the water sizzling in the pot. In his mind, a pink cloud floated. Without realizing it, he slumbered. In his dream, he saw a golden dragon bathing by the Silver River. It was very naughty and kept whipping up the river water with its tail and churning up a gorgeous shower of water beads. Later, perhaps because the dragon flicked its tail on Tianzao's head, he felt a pain there. He opened his eyes and found that he had hit his head on the edge of the oven. The water in the pot had long since boiled, plumes of steam lingering. His parents were not out yet and he could not understand why it took so long to clean his father's back. As he was about to stand up to urge them, he caught sight of a little stream of water flowing quietly towards him. He traced the flow to the "bathroom," from where soft, vague and sweet voices came, too. They must be in the bathtub together, thought Tianzao, and made the water spill over. Water kept flowing out soundlessly beneath the door. Then Tianzao heard the water splashing and the metal bathtub clanking. Blushing, he quickly threw a padded coat over his shoulders and went out to observe the sky.

It was very late. The stars seemed more and more distant from him. He deeply inhaled the cold air, fearing that the growing heat in him might burn him from inside. He wanted very much to sing a children's song but no line of any children's song would come to mind. He did not have Tianyun's talent of composing a song spontaneously. So, he hummed a children's song and walked around the courtyard. The tranquility of the night made the tune extremely moving. He seemed to be enveloped in the music of Heaven. All of a sudden, Tianzao was moved by his own singing. He had never experienced his own voice being so splendid. He almost cried. Just then, the "bathroom" door creaked open, followed by Mother's cheerful, "Tianzao, your turn!"

Tianzao noticed that both his parents' faces were glowing, their eyes filled with happiness as well as shyness, like a cat that had just stolen and eaten food and felt ashamed to face its owner. They dared not look at Tianzao but eagerly helped the boy throw out the dirty bath water. Then they cleaned the bathtub and scooped in clean water.

Tianzao shut the door, removed all of his clothes and switched off the light. Stealthily, he stepped to the window on bare feet and opened the curtain. Then he returned to the bathtub and entered the water slowly. He put his feet in first, which made him quiver. But soon he got used to it. Then he slowly squatted and sat down, relishing the warm feeling of the clean water moving gently on his belly and chest. He laid his head on the edge of the bathtub, looked at the darkness outside the window and saw some eternal stars. He felt those stars flying through the darkness and the window into his bathtub. Like the Chinese honey locust flowers that he had learned about in a textbook, they radiated a light, sweet smell and were ready to help wash away a whole year's worth of dirt from his body. The clean water was wonderful and he had never experienced such comfort and relaxation. He no longer hated the approaching New Year. He wanted to put on his new clothes on New Year's Eve and light the lanterns himself. In addition, he would tell Dawei, upon seeing him again, that he had used clean water for a bath. Besides, the

stars had turned into Chinese honey locust flowers and cascaded
into the clear water in his bathtub.

Translated by Wang Mingjie

图书在版编目（CIP）数据

原野上的羊群/迟子建著;熊振儒等译.—北京:外文出版社,2004
（熊猫丛书）
ISBN 7-119-03664-5

Ⅰ.原... Ⅱ.①迟...②熊... Ⅲ.①中篇小说－作品集－中国－当代－英
文②短篇小说－作品集－中国－当代－英文 Ⅳ.I247.7

中国版本图书馆 CIP 数据核字(2004)第 025607 号

外文出版社网址：
　http://www.flp.com.cn
外文出版社电子信箱：
　info@flp.com.cn
　sales@flp.com.cn

熊猫丛书

原野上的羊群

作　者	迟子建	
译　者	熊振儒等	
责任编辑	陈海燕　李　芳	
封面设计	唐少文	
印刷监制	张国祥	
出版发行	外文出版社	
社　址	北京市百万庄大街 24 号	邮政编码　100037
电　话	(010) 68320579(总编室)	
	(010) 68329514/68327211(推广发行部)	
印　刷	北京市密云春雷印刷厂	
经　销	新华书店/外文书店	
开　本	大 32 开	
印　数	0001—5000 册	印　张　6.5
版　次	2005 年第 1 版第 1 次印刷	
装　别	平	
书　号	ISBN 7-119-03664-5	
	10—E—3608P	
定　价	11.00 元	